From New Y... *bestselling*
author Thea Harrison

**The item should be returned or renewed
by the last date stamped below.**

Dylid dychwelyd neu adnewyddu'r eitem erbyn
y dyddiad olaf sydd wedi'i stampio isod

15 JUN 23

33 24 APR 2023

To renew visit / Adnewyddwch ar
www.newport.gov.uk/libraries

The Chosen

Thea Harrison

The Chosen
Copyright © 2017 by Teddy Harrison LLC
ISBN 13: 978-1-947046-92-4
Print Edition

Cover design by Frauke Spanuth

Chapter One

MAGIC BLEW IN on the winter wind.

As Lily stepped through great iron-bound doors and onto the slippery dock outside, the wind tugged at a lock of her hair. She breathed in deeply. The air was cold and damp, and the briny scent of the sea filled her nostrils.

Margot and the rest of the group followed her, instinctively clustering together for warmth.

Inside Camaeline Abbey, a rotation of priestesses kept a constant web of protections cast over the people who had taken shelter within, as well as the entire island. Camael was the goddess of the Hearth, and the abbey was full of brightness, warmth, companionship, and comfort.

Inside, the magic seemed little more than a nuisance.

Beyond the abbey walls was a different story. Here in the open, the atmosphere felt edgier, more perilous, as if imbued with malice.

Margot paused by Lily's elbow, glancing at the sky.

Damned weather magic, Margot said telepathically. *The caster has a hell of a range. It feels diffuse, lacking a central direction. I can't get a clear read on where it's originating from— can you?*

Over the past six months, she and Margot had developed the habit of carrying on telepathic conversations. As long as they stood within twenty or so feet of each other, they could share insights and compare opinions in complete privacy. It was a useful trait, especially when they were around other people.

Frowning, Lily spoke slowly, feeling her way through the problem. *I would need to travel some distance to be sure, but I think it's likely several weather mages are working together. If they're scattered across the countryside, we wouldn't be able to track the magic back to a single source.*

Several weather mages working to cast banned magic? Margot's jaw tightened. *Sometimes I hate it when you make sense.*

Lily smiled at her ruefully. *You only hate it when you don't like my conclusions.*

True enough. Margot made a face. *Who do you think is behind it, Guerlan or Braugne?*

Tension pinched the back of Lily's neck, threatening to turn into a stress headache. *I truly have no idea. It could be coming from either one—or perhaps even another kingdom is behind it.*

Margot gave her a brief, grim glance. Curtly she gestured to the group, and everyone settled into their assigned positions.

Shivering, Lily tucked the errant strand of hair behind her ear with a gloved hand as she stepped into place. Along with the rest, she turned her attention to the large, squat barge that had launched from the docks of the coastal town of Calles.

The barge's blunt prow crunched through the thin sheets of ice floating on the shallow sea around the island of Camaeline Abbey.

Winter solstice was still a week and a half away. Usually it was a season of celebration, culminating in the Masque of the Gods. This year the weather had turned unseasonably bitter, fueled over the past month by the bouts of magic cast by the unknown mages, and nobody felt like celebrating anything.

Within the next moon, the water between the island and the mainland would be frozen solid for the first time in generations. According to reports, the harvest in all the six kingdoms of Ys had been sparse, and now they faced lethal temperatures.

Lily thought of the small farmsteads dotting the countryside. If the weather mages weren't stopped, many of them would lose much-needed livestock this winter. Probably family members as well.

There was a reason why weather magic was banned. According to international treaty, weather mages were supposed to cast only under royal decree to avert natural disaster.

With Braugne and Guerlan at the brink of war, the implications behind the current weather spells were frightening. Had the king of Guerlan broken treaties and brought a cursed winter to Ys, or had Braugne?

Whoever was behind the weather casting, they had to realize they would be killing people. And if that wasn't bad enough, now the barge that plowed so inexorably toward them carried the infamous Wolf of Braugne himself to the abbey's doorstep, along with a company of his armored soldiers.

They had ridden over the snow-covered horizon just after midday. If they had arrived a little later, they could have walked across the narrow strait. Instead, the soldiers manning the oars had to work to force the barge through the floating sheets of ice.

Lily glanced at her companions. Margot stood at the forefront of the group, watching as the barge drew closer. The young redheaded prime minister of the Camaeline Council was a striking sight in her fur-lined ivory cloak and matching gloves.

Six priestesses stood with Margot, three on either side, the women flanked by armed Defenders of the Hearth. Lily was the middle priestess on the left, just another woman among others.

Unlike Margot, nothing about her stood out. Her cloak was a humble brown, although thank the gods, it was lined and warm enough, and underneath it she wore sturdy winter boots, black trousers, and a thigh-length quilted winter jacket over a plain white tunic.

She was shorter than Margot, and darker, with olive skin, brown eyes, and fine brown hair that refused to grow past her shoulder blades or remain respectably confined by pins. In the summer, she spent as much time as she could outside, often barefoot, and the sun had tanned her to a deep nut brown.

There were a thousand women like her—a hundred thousand—working in farmers' fields, minding shops, and tending to the highborn in their manors and castles.

Pleased with her anonymity, she tucked both hands inside her cloak. She was also pleased to see the other priestesses standing with the same straight-backed pride as Margot, as did the armed Defenders who flanked them.

In direct contrast to their composed appearance, the air churned around the group, filled with images only Lily could see.

What she called the psyches of each individual hovered above and behind their heads, like shadows thrown on a wall.

When she and Margot had been children in the abbey school, Margot's psyche had been that of a gaunt, starving figure, and it had overshadowed her youthful beauty, at least in Lily's eyes. No one else had been aware of it, and as Margot came from a wealthy, noble family, they would have been hard-pressed to believe Lily if she had told them.

Things had changed once Margot accepted the newly created position of prime minister of the abbey council. As soon as she had a place and a function where she was loved and needed, her psyche had filled out. No longer starving, it had turned fierce and protective.

The psyches of the other priestesses and the

Defenders were restless with banked aggression, nerves, and outright fear, but none of it showed in their set faces.

Behind them, the gates to the abbey had been closed and barred in compliance with the Chosen's orders. The gates were set into ancient stone walls that bordered the cliffs at the island's edge.

In the nearest watchtower, members of the abbey council, other priestesses, workers, and townsfolk watched the impending confrontation through tall windows.

The stage for the meeting was set and the audience assembled. If nothing else, this should make interesting theater.

Within a few moments, the barge had neared enough that Lily could make out the features of various soldiers. They stood at parade rest.

The man at their head captured her attention.

The Wolf of Braugne was younger than she had expected, perhaps not yet thirty. He stood with his broadsword drawn, the tip planted in the planks between his feet, both gauntleted hands wrapped around the hilt. His dark hair was windswept, his hard face weathered from the elements.

Stories of him had tumbled across the six kingdoms. They had grown more horrific with each retelling. At midsummer, the Wolf's brother, the ruler and lord of Braugne, had died in a catastrophic avalanche that collapsed a salt mine as well as destroying a portion of the nearby town.

Then the first whispers about the event had reached the abbey, followed by other voices that grew stronger and louder. People started saying the tragic avalanche had been no accident. In an act of pure, calculated evil, the Wolf had murdered his brother, the lord of Braugne, and even now he marched across Ys in a bid for power, executing those who would oppose him, including their children and babies, and burning their homes to the ground.

At first glance, he didn't appear to live up to his legend. He didn't have glowing red eyes, nor did he tower head and shoulders above his men. Lily was a little disappointed, to be honest. She'd been fascinated by the idea of a forked tongue, cloven hooves, and tail.

But no, this was an entirely human-looking man. While he had the strong figure and erect carriage of an experienced soldier, he wasn't exactly handsome either. In fact, he could blend into a crowd on market day and she might brush past without ever giving him a second glance.

Then, as the barge drew close enough to dock, she looked at the Wolf's dark, glittering gaze and thought no.

She would never brush past this man without a second glance. His still figure housed an immensely forceful presence, as if a blazing meteor had been lightly cloaked in flesh. He was a wolf in sheep's clothing, a juggernaut wearing a mild expression as he paused to turn his attention to a tiny principality on his crusade for total domination of Ys.

If the rumors were to be believed.

She drew in a deep breath, and almost without realizing it, she pushed back her hood as she stared at him and his men.

The psyches of the soldiers on the barge roiled and heaved with as much restlessness as the abbey's group on the narrow dock. The images were ghostly and transparent, making it impossible to tell them apart when the physical men stood so close together.

Collectively, they shimmered with fierce, eager energy, as if they were a pack of hunting hounds held on a tight leash, but she couldn't get a specific reading on the Wolf. She would need to see him separate from the others before she could tell anything for sure.

Folding her lips tight, she ran her gaze along the edges of the group, trying at least to glean some information that might be useful.

In direct contrast to Other lands she had read about, most of the populations in Ys were human. Vampyres, the Light and Dark Fae, the Djinn, and others of the Demonkind such as medusae, ghouls, and trolls, were mostly entertaining tales from far distant places. But Lily did see the stern visage and sleek, pointed ears of an Elf among the Braugne soldiers, along with another male who looked as if he might be part Wyr.

As she picked up random details, she narrowed her eyes. Like the waiting group from the abbey, the troops on the barge presented a united front, but not all was well among the Wolf's men.

Lily, put your hood up! Margot exclaimed telepathically. *I don't want him to see your face!*

Lily's reply was distracted. *Hiding under a hood won't offer any protection from what is coming.*

You don't know that! Margot snapped.

Lily glanced at her friend. *With all the visions the goddess has seen fit to send me, actually, I do.*

As Margot's mouth tightened, a rough, powerful voice rolled easily over the water and announced, "Wulfgar Hahn, Protector of Braugne, sends his regards to the Chosen of Camaeline Abbey."

The voice startled her. She had been so intent on trying to sort through the confusing melee of visions and arguing telepathically with Margot, she hadn't noticed that the older, brawny solder had stepped forward until he had spoken.

The soldier bowed to Margot.

Wulfgar Hahn did not bow. He watched with an impassive expression.

"You are mistaken," Margot replied, all ice and hauteur. She was more than just a beautiful face and fiery temperament. She was also an accomplished sorceress, and she held her Power poised to retaliate against any sign of physical aggression. "I am not Camael's Chosen. I am Margot Givegny, prime minister of the Camaeline Council, and if your commander has anything to say to me, he can address me himself."

Scowling, the soldier had opened his mouth to reply

when the Wolf moved to lay one gauntleted hand on the other man's shoulder.

In a deep, pleasant baritone, he said, "I sent word yesterday that I would speak with your Chosen."

Margot looked down her nose at him, and Lily had to bite her lip to suppress a sudden smile. Nobody did supercilious better than Margot when she put her mind to it.

Coldly, Margot replied, "Our Chosen does not respond to tersely worded imperatives from foreigners."

The Wolf dropped his eyelids, shuttering his sharp, dark gaze. It turned his blank, hard expression even more unpredictable.

"Your response is unfortunate." His pleasant baritone acquired bite. "I brought gifts of ancient manuscripts for her, and gold for your abbey. We could have made our business as pleasant as possible."

When he said, "ancient manuscripts," Lily derailed momentarily from her mission to consider them with a pang. But no matter how alluring they might sound, it would have been entirely inappropriate for the Chosen to accept them.

"It is not our duty to make your business *as pleasant as possible* for you," Margot replied. "The abbey has no desire for your gifts."

The Wolf raised one dark eyebrow, and suddenly his unremarkable face became arresting with silken menace. "I have approached you with courtesy—far more courtesy, in fact, than I have shown to any other principality I have met with thus far. You would be wise to take note."

"There is nothing courteous about arriving on our doorstep with an army," Margot said between her teeth.

Wulfgar gestured back to the empty shore. Even the town was silent, as most of the townsfolk had evacuated to the island. "Do you see an army?"

"You may have kept it out of sight, but we still know it's there. Did you think we wouldn't? It's camped on the other side of the woods."

Now it was Wulfgar's turn to speak between his teeth. "I left it behind, again, out of courtesy. I did not arrive on your doorstep with it."

"All the farmlands that surround the town are part of Calles," Margot snapped. "You *are* on our doorstep. You cut down the Chosen's trees and burn it for your firewood. You camp in her fields, hunt her creatures, and drink from her streams without permission. You trespass where you do not belong. If you had meant to be *courteous*, you would have sent word asking permission before you and your army set foot on our land."

They both looked magnificent as they flared with temper. If they had been on stage, they could have made a grand romance out of it, but Lily got the impression the Wolf was only pretending to be angry as his restless gaze roamed over every detail of the scene.

She had no doubt he noticed everything, including the fact that the landing carved from rock upon which the priestesses and Defenders stood was too narrow for any invading force to make effective use of a battering ram on the massive, iron-bound gates.

The two-mile island was bordered by cliffs. It had no beach, only treacherous black rocks, many of which were submerged underwater when the tide rode high. Several generations of stonemasons had worked to build the ancient walls that towered along the cliff's edge. Camaeline Abbey was known for being impregnable and had, on occasion, provided sanctuary to famous figures at different points throughout its long history.

The Wolf and Margot continued to snipe at each other. Their argument faded into the background as Lily angled her head and sidled a small step sideways. Then another. When she bumped shoulders with the priestess on her left, it earned her an uncertain glance.

She'd hoped a shift in perspective might help her gain a clearer vision, but it didn't, and she sighed in frustration. Assessing people's psyches gave her vital clues about a person, but she couldn't get a decent reading on the Wolf, not with the layout of the scene the way it was, especially since she had no other vantage point from which to observe him, and he and his men were limited in their movements as long as they remained on the barge.

Margot would not allow the Wolf of Braugne to step onto the narrow dock, so Lily would need to do something else to get the information she wanted.

Even as she realized that, she snapped to an awareness that something important had happened.

The argument seemed to have turned a corner. She vaguely realized something had been suggested and accepted, but she had been so lost inside her own thoughts she had missed it.

Suddenly Wulfgar's dark, powerful gaze speared her. Taken by surprise at his unexpected attention, she felt skewered, as if she had been stuck on a pin.

He said to Margot, "I agree. I think a liaison from the abbey is exactly what I need." He gestured at Lily. "I'll take that one."

Margot flamed with outrage. "You can't just pick out one of my priestesses like a horse and expect to take her home with you!"

"It's all right, Margot," Lily said. "I don't mind. I'll go with him."

Reaction reverberated through both groups. On the barge, the Wolf raised an eyebrow while his men exchanged glances.

On the dock, Margot whipped around to stare at her. Armor clanked behind Lily as the Defenders took a quick step forward, as if they would prevent her from leaving through physical force.

Why were they all looking at her like that? Scowling, she thought back, teasing out the vague memory of what had just occurred.

Something had been said, along the lines of…

Someone should teach you a lesson.

Oh. Margot had said that.

She hadn't actually *offered* a liaison to the Wolf of

Braugne. She had been sarcastic, but he had leaped on the suggestion to take one anyway, and Lily had blundered right into it.

Well, that was awkward.

Chapter Two

L ILY WAS NO good at diplomacy, and presumably she
had just broken half a dozen protocols by jumping
into the middle of their exchange.

She was, in fact, pretty much a disaster in most
situations.

With a wince, she pinched the bridge of her nose,
and then she gave Margot a sheepish smile.

*For the goddess's sake, what is wrong with you? YOU
CAN'T GO WITH HIM!* Margot shouted telepathically.
Her expression remained rigidly composed, but terror
burned at the back of her gaze.

I think I have to, she replied apologetically.

I'll get you out of it. Margot's eyes flashed. *I'll put my foot
down as prime minister and forbid it.*

*No, Margot—I really think I have to go. I can't read him
when he's standing in the middle of his men, and I don't need to
tell you how important it is we come to understand this man.*

It was, in fact, vital—not only for the abbey, but for
those in Calles who relied upon the abbey's governance
and protection. While she was sorry to put such stress on
her friend, they hadn't stepped outside the abbey walls to

play a safe game. Margot was going to have to deal with it.

Margot pressed her fists against her thighs and looked like she wanted to explode again, but this time she remained silent.

Turning toward the barge, Lily looked at Wulfgar and reached another decision.

She said telepathically to him, *You have a poisoner in your group.*

His hard, dark gaze flared. For the first time since he had arrived, the Wolf of Braugne looked genuinely surprised.

IF WULFGAR WERE the type of man to enjoy a gamble, he would put a thousand gold ducats on the fiery young prime minister holding a blistering telepathic exchange with the petite priestess who had just agreed to be his liaison from Camaeline Abbey.

As the priestess took hold of Jermaine's hand and carefully climbed onto the barge, she nodded a couple of times, shook her head, made a face, and shrugged her shoulders, all as if in acknowledgment to some internal running dialogue, while her expression remained settled and calm.

A corner of his mouth tilted up. Aside from butting in where she didn't belong, this little priestess wasn't any good at schooling her features. That would prove useful. He expected to gather a great deal of information from her.

Margot Givegny speared him with a hard glance. "If you harm a single hair on her head, I'll throw a curse on you that will haunt you for the rest of your life."

Wulfgar's impulse to amusement faded as quickly as it had come. He bit out, "I don't abuse women—unless they try to abuse me first."

His warning was unmistakable, and while she looked daggers at him, she refrained from issuing any other threats. On the barge, Jermaine steadied the priestess, and as she gained her footing, she gave the older man a quick smile that was startling in its sweetness.

He waited until Jermaine released her hand and they had begun their tortuous journey back to shore. Then, when she turned to face him, he snapped telepathically, *Who is it?*

He didn't ask her how she knew. It was common knowledge all Camael's priestesses were witches.

The woman glanced around warily. *I'm not sure. It's hard to tell with all of you standing so close together, and I only got a whisper of it.*

She could be lying. He didn't discount it. She could intend to sow dissension between him and his handpicked men, which might be the whole reason why she agreed to come with him.

But if he had a poisoner in his troops, it would explain so much. It might, in fact, explain everything about the sudden dysentery that plagued his troops and ground their progress to a near halt despite Wulfgar's insistence on maintaining uncompromising sanitary conditions throughout the camps.

He said grimly, *When we reach the docks, I'll have everyone line up. You can walk with me among them and tell me what you find.*

Sudden amusement gleamed in her eyes, and she grinned. Like her first smile, it turned her narrow features into something unusual, even spectacular, and the male in Wulfgar roused to take note.

I have very little experience of a liaison's duties, but I'm fairly certain that's not in the job description, she told him. *While I was happy enough to warn you, I'm not your witch to perform at your beck and call. Your people are your problem.*

We'll see, Wulfgar said in a soft voice that brought the wary expression back to her features.

For someone who had never previously had much time for witches, recent events had conspired to make him intensely interested in utilizing their services. He just needed to find out what this one wanted. Everyone wanted something, and it was always better to try a touch of honey first in case it eased one's path.

But if honey—or in this case, ancient manuscripts and gold—failed, he would have to find other methods to employ.

Because he would not quit. He would not fail. And he would not turn back.

As the barge made the short journey back to the mainland, he sheathed his sword, crossed his arms, and studied his new acquisition in frowning silence.

She did not seem to be discomfited by his attention. That was unusual. Given enough time under the pressure of his regard, most people's composure fractured to some extent.

Dominant personalities turned belligerent. Others grew fearful and anxious. Nearly all of them revealed something useful about themselves.

This one, however, ignored him with apparent ease. Turning to face the shore, she stole sidelong glances at the tall soldiers who, to a man, towered over her petite frame.

He cocked an eyebrow at Jermaine who gave him a sidelong grin. Points to her for surprising him back at the abbey dock. Points again for weathering his attention with no visible signs of stress or... any other reaction that he could tell.

Once the barge was moored, Jermaine climbed to the icy dock, moving with the nimble grace of a man half his age. Turning, he extended his hand again to the priestess, who accepted it with a quick smile of thanks, and he helped her to climb out safely.

When she stood solidly on the dock, Wulfgar vaulted out of the barge. Her gaze flickered as she surveyed him, and her expression changed. Something about him had finally caught her attention and made her react while his death stare, as Jermaine liked to jokingly call it, had done nothing.

What had she noticed? He decided he would enjoy figuring out what made her react. And enjoy figuring out how to use it to his best advantage.

Turning, he strode down the icy dock to the shoreline. As he stepped onto land, he paused to frown at the collection of ice-crusted metal contraptions that rested between the bars of a long metal stand.

They had puzzled him when he had first arrived at the dock. Now he had someone he could ask for an explanation.

As the priestess stopped beside him, he gestured to the metal things. "What are those paired wheels for?"

She glanced at him in surprise. "Those are bicycles… my lord? I'm sorry, I'm afraid I don't know how to address you."

He replied, "*Commander* will suffice. What are bicycles?"

"Bicycles are an Earth invention that work successfully here in Ys. I forgot—there aren't any crossover passageways in Braugne, are there?"

"No," he said, his manner turning terse. "Only those who live near a crossover passageway and reap the economic benefits they bring can afford to forget something like that. But we who live in Braugne always remember. The nearest crossover passageway is halfway across the continent from us."

Her gaze widened with such shocked dismay he felt almost as if he had physically struck her.

"Of course, you're correct," she said. "I apologize—I didn't mean to cause offense. When I was a small child, I lived in an area that didn't have any crossover passageways nearby either, so I understand what you mean."

An unaccustomed sense of contrition bit at his conscience. Impatient with himself, he shook his head. "I am the one who should apologize. You didn't mean anything by your remark."

"You're right though. There are three crossover passageways nearby. Two of them lead to France and another to northern Spain, so Calles has a lot of imports from Earth. They have made our lives better in many ways." She stepped to the nearest metal contraption to lay a hand on it. "Take the bicycle. You sit here, on the saddle, and while you pump these two pedals with your feet, you can steer where you want to go with the handlebars. You have to learn how to balance, so it takes practice at first."

He watched her closely. Her expression lit up when she was talking, and there it was again, that unusual, even spectacular something. "What interests you about them?"

She brightened further. "Most people can travel farther and faster on a bicycle than they can on foot, and they are far cheaper to own than a horse. It doesn't get sick, and you don't have to worry about the cost of feed or if you have enough field to pasture it. This summer the Chosen paid a subsidy to the town blacksmith to make them for some of the poorer farms nearby. When they attach a small wagon behind the rear wheel, they can bring their goods to market in town."

Ah, yes. The quiet town.

But he would get to that in a minute.

"So, having a bicycle makes their lives better." He considered the contraptions thoughtfully.

"Yes, and they're also fun to ride once you get the hang of it. The children love them." She frowned at the ice-packed dirt road that led into town. "Although they're not so easy to ride in winter, and the whole of Ys would need to have a far better system of roadways for them to be viable for long-distance travel. Still, bit by bit, we're working on making the roads around the town better."

"I see." She clearly didn't realize how much she gave away about herself when she talked about a subject she felt so passionate about.

"Perhaps you might like to take a bicycle back to Braugne with you."

"Perhaps so." Reluctant to destroy the fragile rapport they had established, he didn't tell her he had no intention of returning to Braugne anytime soon.

Instead, he turned to Lionel and ordered, "Major, set a watch on the dock and notify me immediately if there's any movement from the abbey. Jermaine and Gordon, you stay with me and the priestess. The rest of you, return to camp."

"Yes, Commander," Lionel said.

As he set a pair of soldiers on watch, Wulfgar turned back to catch the priestess studying him. The icy wind had whipped her cheeks into a pleasing rosy color.

She told him, "If you might trust what I tell you, it would save your men a lot of effort in this cold. Nobody on that island is going anywhere while you're here."

"You may be right." He studied the island with a narrowed gaze. "Or they may change their minds. And my men are not here to be spared any effort."

At that her expression turned sour, but she shrugged.

Perhaps she didn't want to destroy the fragile rapport either. Or perhaps it was no matter to her.

Either way, he didn't think she had meant anything underhanded by her suggestion. It was probably just as she had said. The people sheltering on the island wouldn't need to come to the mainland for supplies.

From the accounts he had read, the long-dead architects of the abbey had made good use of every inch of land. They would have vegetable gardens, fruit trees, fields of grain, and plentiful water. No doubt farm animals too, at the very least chickens and goats, and probably sheep as well.

The island would be well fortified, and there were only two gateways that offered an entrance through the fortress walls. The first was the public dock they had just left, which was wide enough for three or four barges to dock but too narrow to allow for all of them to unload at once.

In one text he had examined, the writer described a second dock that faced seaward. Smaller and more private, it mirrored the public dock in almost every detail, with a narrow ledge made even more slippery and

treacherous by waves from the open sea and a stairway
that cut into the cliff that was barred by a heavy, iron-
bound door.

A battering ram was useless in those conditions, and
even if either of those doors were breached, it would
only take a few fighters to defend the stairways. They
could hold off an invasion indefinitely while an attacking
force would have to contend with the confined space,
the narrow ledge, and the sea itself, along with whatever
those manning the walls saw fit to throw down on them.

He and his men could climb those cliffs and scale the
walls. Braugne was a difficult, mountainous country, and
most soldiers were taught how to climb before they
reached manhood.

But that kind of climb would be too hard and slow
to gain any real purchase in battle. It would involve
hammers, pitons, and rope. The abbey had a few blind
spots on the towers that faced seaward, but he wouldn't
be able to get enough of his men up the walls before
they were pelted with rocks from above, or worse,
boiling water or oil. Inevitably, they would be swept into
the sea.

Meanwhile, the abbey could survive for years under
siege, definitely for far longer than all but the most
stubborn of armies.

If they were under siege, they wouldn't have access
to the outside world, either to their precious crossover
passageways or to the rest of Ys, and sooner or later, that
isolation would chafe. But still, the only thing they were

truly vulnerable to was treachery.

And the only way they could be taken was from within.

Chapter Three

H E TURNED TOWARD Calles. It was time to survey the silent town.

"Come," he said.

The priestess joined him, and Jermaine and Gordon fell into step behind them.

As they walked the short distance to town, she pulled her hood up, but she didn't complain about his insistence on exploring the town in inclement weather. He found himself liking her just a little bit.

Clasping his hands behind his back, he matched his longer stride to hers. "What is your name?"

"Lily."

"Do you have a title? In Braugne we call Camaeline priestesses *my lady*."

"That has always sounded so fancy to me. I was a foundling, so I'm not used to it. Please just call me Lily."

He could hear the smile in her voice, and briefly, he wanted to lift her hood away so he could see that spectacular something in her expression again.

Frowning at the unwelcome impulse, he said, "You didn't have to agree to this. You could have gone back to a cozy abbey fire. Your prime minister certainly wanted you to."

Ruefully, she replied, "Margot is very protective."

"Yet, when I brought up the subject of taking a liaison, I don't think she had an objection to giving me a priestess. She just didn't want it to be you." He let her mull that over for a moment as he watched her closely, intensely interested in how she would respond next.

Then she sighed heavily enough he could hear it despite the wind. "She and I have known each other for most of our lives. She tormented me when we were small, but now that we've grown past all that, she seems to want to make up for it by keeping me wrapped in wool and tucked away in a drawer."

He almost smiled. It was a good deflection. She was careful about what she said, confessing to a small truth without giving away too much.

He said, "You became friends."

She laughed. "It still sounds funny to admit, but yes, much to my surprise, we've become friends."

"I like your laugh." While his tone was brusque, he spoke the truth. Her laugh sounded warm and infectious. If she were a courtesan, he might have purchased a night with her based on her laugh alone.

When she peeked around the edge of her hood at him, the wary expression was back in her eyes. "Thank you."

They had reached the town's main street, and as they walked he studied the closed shops and dark houses. In a few of the shops' windows, he saw luxury items.

Chocolates and scented soaps and gourmet packaged foods from Earth. In one shop window, jars of caviars were stacked in a pyramid between bunches of roses that had been cleverly fashioned out of crimson velvet.

When he saw jars of caviar, he remembered the single taste he'd had once, spooned onto a flat salt bread called a cracker, and his mouth watered.

Much of Earth's technologies didn't work in what they called Other lands, like Ys, where magic took prominence. Most weapons, combustible engines, and the like were useless, if not outright dangerous, but from what he had experienced, there wasn't a single thing wrong with the food.

After walking a few blocks, he said, "Most of the town's population is on the island, I take it."

"Yes, Commander." She turned businesslike. "The town council urged everyone to evacuate, but a few refused."

"Who remains?"

"There are two brothels who anticipate earning some of your men's money, along with a couple of inns that remain open to any travelers who may desire a warm bed under a roof as a change from the hardship of a winter camp." She paused, then said evenly, "The rest of us are simply hoping you don't abuse the women, loot or ransack the businesses, or requisition everyone's homes without their permission."

He stopped walking, abruptly angry with the

townsfolk cowering on the island, angry with their blasted Chosen who had decided to play this roundabout game instead of meeting with him openly, and angry with everything else about the miserable, freezing day.

Hold on to your temper, Wulf, Jermaine said. *This isn't her fault.*

Pivoting, he glared at the other man. Then he strode back to the shop that had the jars of caviar in the window, his long legs making short work of the distance. Stripping off his gauntlets, he dug into his pocket for tools and picked the lock on the shop door.

Lily had followed him, her posture stiff with outrage, but she said nothing when he thrust open the door and strode into the shadowy interior.

By the door, Jermaine sighed. "You might as well step inside too, my lady. This might take a few minutes."

"The shop is not open," she bit out.

"No," he agreed. "But there is also no reason to stand outside in this wind until we absolutely must."

After a moment's hesitation, she stepped inside, and Jermaine and Gordon followed.

Wulfgar ignored them. There were twenty small jars of caviar along with a couple of different kinds of salt bread. He swept all the jars together and dumped them on the counter.

He preferred the salt bread made in Ys to the kind he had sampled from Earth, and he grabbed several packets to toss them beside the caviar, then selected a couple of bottles of wine. He had always wondered what chocolate might taste like, so he grabbed some packages, and then a strange metal container nearby caught his attention.

Picking it up, he frowned at the graphic and sounded out the strange words written in English. "Ch-ef Bouy…"

Lily snapped, "It's called Chef Boyardee. The shop stocks it especially for the Chosen, who gets a hankering for it sometimes."

"Well then. If it's good enough for her, it's good enough for me." He added a can to the pile. "Gordon, Jermaine, is there anything you want from in here?"

"Not at the moment, Commander. Perhaps later." Gordon spoke politely while Jermaine just looked at him in exasperation.

"Fine." He said to Gordon, "Tally up the cost, and leave the coin in a jar behind the counter. When you're done, take everything back to my tent."

"Yes, sir."

While Gordon busied himself, Wulf turned to Lily, who stared at him with wide eyes. She had pushed her hood back. The friction caused fine strands of dark hair to float around her head in a delicate nimbus.

"No matter how long I remain camped in Calles, that coin will remain untouched behind the counter." With an effort, he kept his voice quiet and even, but his anger still burned through. "The shopkeeper may choose to remain on the island, but presumably he or she would still like to earn a living. If any of my troops want to buy anything, they will add their coin to mine. There will be no looting.

Under my command, the punishment for rape is death. Since embarking on this campaign, I haven't had to carry out that sentence once."

"I see," she said, her voice quiet.

"While we are at it, I also did not assassinate the lord of Braugne. That act was committed by someone else." His gaze burned with a steady, banked rage. "He was not only my half brother, he was my closest friend, and I will avenge his death if it takes me the rest of my life."

As he had spoken, pink color had washed over her cheeks. Clearly floundering, she opened her mouth and closed it again. When she finally spoke, her voice was subdued. "We have heard tales of other things."

"I'm all too aware of the stories being told," he said between his teeth. "I've also seen the bodies left butchered in homesteads, and the burned fields. None of those atrocities have been committed by me or my men."

"I'm sorry for your loss." Her reply was even softer than before.

This time he refused to let remorse get a foothold. "Now, if that will be all, I've got other things to attend to." He looked at Gordon. "Take her back to camp with you."

"Yes, Commander."

LILY DECIDED SHE wasn't going to get offended at being taken back to camp along with the commander's purchases as if she were another of his possessions.

She'd already caused enough trouble for one afternoon.

Retreating into the shelter of her hood, she walked to the encampment beside Gordon. He was taciturn, and she made no attempt to break the silence.

Every passionate word the Wolf had spoken had rung with truth. He shouldn't have broken into the shop of course, but she suspected he had done it in part because he had lost his temper. When he had left her, he and Jermaine had headed toward the closest inn where golden light gleamed in the windows, shining brightly in the frigid, sullen day.

She chewed her lip. What were they doing, and why had he sent her ahead to the camp instead of keeping her with him?

Maybe they were securing rooms for the night. Maybe they were hiring women, and her presence would have been, well, cumbersome.

At that thought, she pulled a face. All in all, it was best she hadn't joined them. The gods only knew, every time she opened her mouth, she threatened to let out something she shouldn't. The less opportunity she had for creating more headaches for everyone, the better.

Cook fires dotted the landscape of tents that covered the valley up to the edge of the forest. It was a sobering sight. There must be thousands of troops. She didn't see any cattle, which puzzled her at first, but when she heard a whinny from the direction of the trees, she realized they were using the forest for the shelter it offered their animals from the wind.

Among the orderly rows, the commander's tent was unmistakable, larger than the others with two guards at the flaps. She swiftly scanned the encampment but could find no hint of the weather magic which had died down a while ago.

Once at the commander's tent, Gordon lifted a flap and gestured for her to precede him. Uncomfortable and fascinated at once, she stepped through the opening to discover a pleasant surprise.

The interior was filled with light and warmth. Thick rugs covered the ground, and woolen hangings around the tent walls provided relief from the winter chill. Braziers warmed the interior and provided the light.

To one side a sitting area was made up of chairs constructed of leather stretched on wooden frames. A large table of planks set on wooden blocks dominated the other side. There were papers strewn over the top, along with maps.

Aside from the colors woven into the patterned rugs and hangings, it was all very plain, but overall the interior was much more comfortable than she had expected and much less intimate than she had feared. A woolen hanging separated the tent into two spaces. It had been tied back, and just visible on the other side was the edge of a neatly made bed.

Inside, she quickly grew overheated and removed her cloak. Gordon unloaded the bag of purchases and stacked everything neatly at one end of the table. She hovered nearby.

The maps and the papers beckoned her. She wanted to rifle through them, but Gordon positioned himself near the tent opening where he watched her steadily with an impassive expression.

His psyche was another matter. When she gave Gordon a polite smile, the shadowy figure over his head glared at her with unmistakable enmity.

There was just no making friends with some people. She had learned a long time ago to mask her reactions to the psyches around her… mostly.

She asked, "Might the commander have something I could look at while I wait?"

After a moment, the soldier nodded to a pile of books that were stacked on a wooden stump by one of the chairs in the sitting area. Wandering over, she picked up the books.

One was a history of Camaeline Abbey. Another was a set of biographies following the lineage of the Chosens. The Wolf of Braugne had done his homework before arriving.

Flipping through the biographies, she saw the last penned entry was about Raella Fleurise and made no mention of the new Chosen. She wasn't surprised. The date at the beginning of the book meant it had been created before Raella's death in the spring.

Unexpected tears pricked Lily's eyes. Raella had been elderly, and she had died peacefully of natural causes, her husband and family by her side. One couldn't ask for a better ending, but in many ways, she had been the mother Lily'd never had, and she thought she would feel Raella's absence for the rest of her life.

Closing the book, she set it back on the stack with the others. Then, selecting a chair at random, she settled and prepared to wait for the commander to finish his business in town.

He wasn't gone long.

She had untied the fastenings of her quilted jacket and drifted into a doze when voices sounded outside the tent. As she jerked awake, the flap lifted, bringing a blast of cold air along with the Wolf. Jermaine followed at his heels.

Instantly, the interior of the spacious tent felt much smaller—too small, in fact, and far more intimate than it had a few moments ago. As Lily stirred, Wulfgar's sharp eyes took in everything at a single glance, her position near one of the braziers, Gordon's stolid presence, the neat stack of store-bought goods.

As his attention lingered on the maps and papers at the other end of the table, the devil took hold of Lily's mouth.

"Curiosity is a sin," she said, keeping her tone pious. "Of course I wanted to read all of it."

His dark gaze snapped back to her, and he laughed. She wasn't sure which of them was more surprised by it.

Smiling, Jermaine collected the papers and rolled up the maps. Wulfgar unbuckled his sword belt and laid the sword on the table. As Gordon took his cloak, breastplate, and gauntlets, he ordered, "Bring us some mulled wine."

"Yes, sir." Bowing his head, Gordon stepped out, followed by Jermaine.

With no one else present to buffer the impact of Wulfgar's personality, the interior of the tent shrank even farther in size.

Underneath the breastplate he had worn leather padding, and he undid the fastenings as he strode toward the brazier beside her. As he pulled the padding off and tossed it onto a chair, she saw that he wore a black linen shirt that was open at the strong column of his tanned throat.

Power coursed through the air. The power of his personality, the goddess's Power.

She fought the urge to back away, fought to stand steady in the face of it.

His psyche… his psyche was the shadow of a wolf, huge in size, and it crouched as if preparing to spring, its attention unwaveringly on her.

This was unmistakably one of the two men she had seen in visions for the past several years. She had known he was coming to Calles for some time, but now that he was here, she felt utterly at a loss as to what to do about him.

Holding his scarred hands over the glowing coals of the fire, he said, pleasantly enough, "I presume you have assessed the encampment. That is one of the reasons why you agreed to come, is it not?"

Cautiously, she said, "It is, and yes, I have."

"Did you learn what you wanted to know?"

"I'm not sure yet," she admitted. "We at the abbey have a lot of disparate pieces of information, and I don't understand how it all fits together."

He turned to face her fully. It was a simple shift in posture, but the tiny hairs at the back of her neck rose in response.

Perhaps unwisely, she added, "I didn't sense any weather mages in your camp."

Destiny was like a golden river, sweeping them all to an unknown shore. Visions crowded at the edge of her eyesight until she wasn't sure what she might say or do.

Margot was right to be terrified of letting her loose from the abbey. Lily wasn't fit to go anywhere by herself.

His hard mouth drew tight. "That's because there aren't any. Did you really believe I might be behind the intensification of this early winter?"

Forcing herself to stay anchored in the here and now, she lifted a shoulder. "Try to imagine things from our point of view. You know the terrible things we've heard about your approaching army. An invading force that would torch farms and execute people might also use the weather as a weapon to subdue a populace."

He shook his head with a snort. "A decision like that would cripple my troops as much as it would anyone else around me. No general in their right mind launches a campaign in the dead of winter—and right now it has turned so unseasonably cold, that is, in effect, what we're facing if those weather mages are not stopped. They are trying to force me to halt."

As she listened, she pressed the knuckles of her folded hands against her lower lip. What he said made undeniable sense. "Do you have witches in your army?"

"None with the kind of skills that the Camaeline priestesses have," he growled. "Why do you think I came with gifts of manuscripts and gold? If I made a habit of giving away large sums of wealth to everyone I met, I'd have no funds left to pay for my army. My witches have been fending off the weather attacks as best they can, but there are too few of them. They're exhausted, and we're still camped in the open."

The fine skin around her eyes crinkled as she winced. "You need shelter."

"Yes. That's why I stayed in town. I met with the inn owners and brothel keepers to negotiate terms so my troops can take time inside in rotation. Tomorrow Jermaine and I are going to hunt for our poisoner among the soldiers who were on the barge this afternoon. I also want to negotiate with Calles's townsfolk for the rental of their homes. You can take the details of my offer back to the abbey in the morning."

She frowned. "I can try."

His expression turned impatient. "Since they're hiding on the island anyway, there's no reason they can't make good coin while they're at it. My gold is as good as any other."

"You have a point, but it's more complicated than the townsfolk just collecting rent while they're absent from their houses." Pinching the bridge of her nose with thumb and forefinger, she tried to think through the issue like Margot would. "I sympathize with the position you are in, but it's similar to how it would look if the Chosen had accepted your gifts. There's the politics of it, the appearance of support. Calles would, in effect, be declaring sides."

"Calles is going to have to pick a side," he said bluntly. "Guerlan or Braugne. There is no question of that."

As he spoke, Lily felt a breath of air along her skin, as though she were being brushed by the cloak of someone immense walking by, and she knew the goddess was near.

He was right, of course. She had seen this coming since she was a child.

Like the rocks and sand that shifted on the shore with the tide, the visions had varied over the years, until recently they had become fixed into a pattern of unshifting dichotomy.

A bitter winter after a lean harvest. The kingdoms of Ys filled with unrest.

A darkening over the land, like the sun dying. The clash of swords.

Two men, a wolf and a tiger, slamming together in mortal combat. One of them had an insatiable hunger that would grind Ys to dust.

And the fall of Calles. In every shifting vision, that was the one part that remained immutable.

"No," she whispered, her heart aching. "We can't remain neutral, can we? Even though we might wish it."

"You look like you've seen a ghost."

She forced the images away and plastered a smile on her face. "No ghosts here, only an uncertain path to the future."

His gaze was too discerning for comfort. Then, deliberately, he lightened the mood. "The future is going to have to wait for a few hours. I haven't had lunch and I'm starving."

Pivoting, he strode back to the table, picked up a jar of caviar, and twisted off the lid. Tearing open a packet of salt bread, he unsheathed the knife at his waist, scooped some of the caviar onto the flat wafer, and popped it in his mouth. Closing his eyes briefly, he chewed, pleasure evident in his strong features.

Watching him consume the delicacy with such sensual enjoyment made her skin tingle. It was… erotic. Heat washed over her skin at the word.

"Have you ever tasted caviar?" he asked.

"No." She looked at the fire in the brazier. "I haven't tried most things in that shop. Imports from Earth are expensive."

His broad hand appeared in her line of vision, holding out a wafer with caviar. "Here."

Surprise flared. Her gaze flew to his face. "Oh… thank you! But I couldn't."

He frowned. "Don't be ridiculous. Take it."

"I…" As his frown grew fierce, her protest died.

Accepting the wafer from his long fingers, she nibbled at it curiously. Briny pearls of flavor and salted crunch filled her mouth.

A gleam of amusement sparked in his dark eyes. "You have an expressive face, but I can't read what it is saying right now. What do you think?"

She swallowed before she replied. "Honestly, I'm not sure. I don't have much of a taste for fishy flavors. It's very interesting. Intense."

"It's fabulous. Have more. No? The chocolate then." Before she could protest, he tore open one of the chocolate bars, broke it into pieces, and offered one to her. As she wavered, his expression turned suddenly wise. "You've had chocolate before, and you like it."

"I love it," she said on a little moan.

She felt agonized with indecision. Was it appropriate for her to accept it? She wasn't a reliable source on what was appropriate at the best of times.

And she could smell it, the chocolate. It smelled like heaven.

"For the gods' sake, woman. What's the matter? If you love it, then why are you holding back? It's just food, not manuscripts and gold." He took a piece and teased it between her lips.

Shocked by his sudden intrusion into her personal space, she felt her mouth drop open and then her tongue came into contact with the sweet. This was ridiculous. She couldn't spit it out now. She'd licked it.

Meeting his gaze, she burst out laughing, cupping her

hands underneath her chin to keep from accidentally dropping the piece.

He grinned. Above his head, his wolf grinned too.

Behind her came a rush of frigid air, and both she and the commander turned.

Gordon had entered, carrying a tray with two goblets and a pewter jug. His expression remained as impassive as ever, but as he took in their laughing faces, his psyche turned sharper, darker. When he offered her the contents on the tray, his psyche hissed at her.

Carefully, she kept from reacting. As she took a goblet, she scanned both him and the drinks he carried.

Was Gordon the poisoner she had sensed back at the dock?

Chapter Four

N O, HER WINE "felt" safe enough to drink, and this man was too straightforward for poison. She was all but sure of it. If he was going to kill someone, he would go for the throat. Or the heart.

Poison took a stealthy patience, iron nerves, and the ability to lie—or at least misdirect well enough—to someone with truthsense under pressure.

"Thank you," she said as she accepted it.

He gave her a short nod and handed Wulfgar the other goblet, then set the jug on the table. "Will that be all, my lord?"

"No, you might as well order an early supper," Wulfgar said. "Have Jada bring two plates for the priestess and me. I want you to prepare quarters for her. After we eat, we'll get her settled for the night. I want her close by."

Once again, he was disposing of her as if she were a possession. Frowning, she opened her mouth, but Gordon spoke first.

"Shall I prepare my tent?" he asked. "Since it's beside yours, it would be easy enough for the guards to keep watch over her as well. I can make a pallet for myself in here, if that would suffice. Or, if you would prefer, I'm sure Jermaine will be amenable if I bunk with him. You'll have to send for me if you want something."

"Go ahead and bunk with Jermaine," Wulfgar told him. "Once supper arrives, I won't need your services until morning. And be sure to add another brazier and plenty of fuel to your tent. Extra bedding as well."

"Very good, sir." Bowing his head, Gordon slipped out.

Sucking a tooth sourly, Lily contemplated the contents in her goblet. When Wulfgar turned to her, she could feel his attention, almost as if it were a physical touch.

"Now what does that expression imply?" He sounded amused.

She took a sip, more to procrastinate for a few moments than from any real desire to drink. She knew what Margot would do—Margot would fume at the preemptory treatment and probably start another argument, but that didn't seem productive.

The warm wine was an explosion of flavor, spiced with cinnamon, cloves, and orange. After she swallowed, she said cautiously, "I'm not used to being talked about as if I'm not in the room, or disposed of like a... a trunk full of books. But I'm also not experienced at being a liaison for anybody, so..."

"Point taken. Next time I'll include you in the discussion." He took a seat, letting his long legs sprawl, and drank wine. "What do you see your role as?"

She shrugged. "I'm not a servant, but I'm not an official ambassador either. I—We—Basically Margot told me to try to behave myself and explain anything you needed to have explained."

"And assess my camp. Assess me." His gaze was penetrating. She felt as she had back on the dock, that he was taking in every detail about her and probably seeing more than she wanted him to see. That thought brought a wash of warmth to her face.

"Yes," she admitted.

"So… assess me." He gestured at the empty seat across from him. "What do you see?"

Moving to take the seat, she studied him. The black linen shirt revealed the strong, clean lines of his throat and the swell of muscle at the top of his pectoral. Even in such a relaxed pose he conquered the space, the tip of his boots almost reaching hers. His dark hair fell on his forehead, giving his hard features a somewhat boyish look.

No, that wasn't the right word. There was nothing boyish about the dangerous man lounging so casually across from her.

Roguish. That was the word. The disheveled hair seemed to bely the discipline he had shown so far. He was amused by her.

She said, "You carry a great deal of rage, and you're driven to accomplish what you have set out to do. It couldn't wait until the spring—you needed to take action immediately. You won't turn back or turn aside. But you're disciplined about it, and despite your anger you're thinking about the welfare of your men. From what little I've seen, you have a code that you are determined to live by, at least when you can. I haven't seen enough of you to know what might happen to that code when you're under duress."

As she spoke, the roguish gleam in his gaze faded, and she fell silent, suddenly uncertain. Maybe she had read him wrong. Maybe he hadn't really wanted to hear what she thought. But if he hadn't, then why had he asked her?

She wanted to flail. She was no good in *any* social situation.

"Don't stop now." He tossed back the last of the wine in his goblet. "You just got started."

So that meant he truly did want to hear the rest of it. Right?

Biting her lip, she continued. "You're not above seizing every opportunity that comes your way, and you never stop thinking about how to turn things to your advantage. You're a strategist. I'm no good at strategy, so I would be wary of playing chess with you because you're always thinking four steps ahead. Your words carried a ring of truth when you said you did not kill the lord of Braugne. You haven't said specifically who you believe did, but it is clear you see the king of Guerlan as your antagonist, so naturally there are inferences to be drawn. And yet this campaign of yours is about so much more than just avenging your lord's death. You have the soul of a conqueror." She hesitated, and then made herself say the rest of it. "I don't think you will rest until you have taken all of Ys under your rule."

As she finished, he watched her with the same hard, grim expression he had worn on the barge. Unpredictable. Uncompromising. The wolf in his psyche watched her as well, tension in its figure as if it were about to pounce.

He said in a soft, even voice, "That was unexpected."

✧　✧　✧

WULF WATCHED AS Lily bit her lip.

She was a study in delicacy—the narrow features, the slender bones underneath thin skin, the fine hair that had slipped out of its confinement and tumbled to her shoulders in a gleaming fall of silk. Slender fingers wandered along the rim of her goblet, and the light from the fire in the brazier revealed a subtle play of shadows on her throat muscles as she swallowed.

He had known, and appreciated, many beautiful women in his life, but Lily was more than merely beautiful.

She was fascinating.

Unlike fashionable ladies who protected their skin, she still carried a tan from the summer's sun, but that didn't prevent him from seeing every fluctuation of betraying color in her cheeks.

She asked, wryly, "Too much?"

"Not at all. To be honest, I didn't think you had it in you." He set his goblet aside. "I'm beginning to understand why your prime minister went along with your coming with me."

Someone who was not watching her as closely as he might not have noticed how she stilled at that.

But he did, and he waited for any confessions she might see fit to tell him.

Bending her face to her drink, she took another sip and asked, "What do you mean?"

He suppressed a smile. She used that thick, unwieldy goblet as if she could truly hide behind it.

The naivete of that was amusing. After every astute observation she had just made, she should realize nothing could hide her from him, not now that he had fixed his attention upon her.

He said, "You might be clumsy in social situations, but you more than make up for it by how observant you are." He paused a beat, then deliberately switched to a lighter tone. "I think you should eat more chocolate."

Sitting straight, her gaze flew wide, and the memory of laughter woke her face to that bright, spectacular something again. "No, thank you. I-I'm sure I shouldn't… I probably shouldn't have eaten that first piece, except you shoved it in my mouth, so what was I supposed to do? It's too expensive to spit on your rugs."

"I could do it again," he said, bringing his voice down low, almost to a whisper. "I could press a piece right between your lips, and what would you do then?"

She met his gaze, her expression a delicious concoction of scandalized rejection, helpless desire, and that suppressed laughter that flitted like a white butterfly on an unpredictable wind.

An invisible connection throbbed between them, unexpectedly powerful and undeniable.

He had meant to tease her. He had not expected to find this small, awkward woman sexy.

Moving slowly so he didn't frighten her, he pulled out of his lounging position and stood as he asked, still in that low voice, "Should I tell you what I see about you?"

The hint of laughter vanished. "I don't think that would be a productive use of our time together, Commander."

He was almost sorry to see her laughter go. Almost, except this consternation was even more delicious than anything else.

But her attempt at a more formal address was irritating. "Don't call me Commander. Call me Wulf." Scooping the opened bar of chocolate from the table, he strolled toward her. "What, in your opinion, would be a productive use of our time together?"

"Shouldn't we continue talking about Calles, and Braugne, and what might be the best way to–to… to…" As he knelt in front of her, she leaned back in her seat, her widened gaze bouncing from his face to the chocolate he held in one hand. Coaxing the goblet out of her hands, he set it to one side.

"To what, Lily?" he asked, breaking a piece of chocolate off from the bar. "To strengthen relations between us?"

The tantalizing color rushed under her fine skin, and she turned scolding. "You should not be so–so..."

"I should not be so what, Lily?" Leaning toward her, he teased the plump edge of her bottom lip with the chocolate as he whispered, "I think you might know what I intend to do. Tell me yes or tell me no."

As he looked deeply into her eyes, he could tell she had begun to wonder if he was still talking about the chocolate. She opened her mouth, those delicate, fine lips trembling on the verge of a response.

In that moment, he felt desire as keen as a sword thrust. Slipping the chocolate between her parted lips, he stroked it along her tongue. After hesitating, her lips closed on the candy and she sucked it.

He took a deep, quiet breath as his groin tightened. Oh yes. Now they had begun an entirely different conversation.

The tent flap lifted, and a tall, thin man wrapped in a cloak shouldered his way inside. It was Jada, carrying in the food tray.

At the intrusion, Lily jerked away from Wulf, wiping her mouth with the back of one hand. Smoothly, he straightened from his kneeling position. An experienced campaigner knew when to press forward and when to retreat.

Jada had frozen halfway in. His quick gaze bounced

from Lily to Wulf, then to the laden tray he balanced.

"For the gods' sake, man!" Wulf snapped. "Don't stand there with the tent flap open. Come in!"

"Of course, my lord!" The other man jerked forward, and the tent flap fell behind him, blocking out the bitter cold. "I'll just lay out the supper and be on my way."

Wulf glanced back at Lily. She had snatched up a book and opened it, appearing to study the text intently while red color bloomed in her cheeks. He bit back a sudden urge to laugh.

He couldn't remember when he had last wanted a woman as badly as he wanted this one or when he had last been so entertained.

We're not done with our discussion, he told her, his telepathic voice silken with intent.

She snapped the book shut and grabbed at another. *I don't know what you're talking about, Commander.*

Not 'Commander.' Wulf.

Oh fine—Wulf! I shouldn't have eaten that second piece of chocolate either. I'm probably going to hell for it.

What are you talking about? He wanted to laugh. *What is this hell you refer to, and why would you go there for eating chocolate?*

She hunched her shoulders. *The religions of the Elder Races don't really have a hell, do they? It's an Earth concept. It's where you go when you've been very bad.*

And how are you being very bad? Is it the politics of it? The appearance of support? All the evidence of any chocolate transgression has melted away. He couldn't resist and strolled over to her.

Even though she never looked up from her book, her breathing quickened as he drew near. She was as aware of him as he was of her.

Coming up behind her, he bent to whisper in her ear, "Relax. I give you my word, no one need ever know what transpires in this tent."

He watched her profile in the golden light, the way she licked her lips, the lacy shadow that lay on her cheeks from the curve of her dark eyelashes. She looked at him out of the corner of her eye, and he almost took her in his arms right then and there, despite the manservant behind them who lay the supper dishes out on the table.

He had no time for this. For her.

His brother's killer sat on Guerlan's throne. Weather mages were working constantly to threaten his army, and he had ambitions. Yes, by the gods, she had been correct. He did have ambitions.

This woman didn't factor into any of his goals or schemes. And yet he was drawn to dally, if but for a moment or two, to share warmth on a bitter winter's night, to smile at the multitude of ways she managed to be so transparent and yet still surprise him.

To discover the taste of her mouth, the sensation of her body against his.

In the fleeting privacy created by his bigger body as he stood between her and the manservant, he reached around her shoulder to lightly trace the satiny skin of her neck, the line of her jaw. He felt her swallow at his touch, and he was so rock hard from that tiny interaction he had to move.

Move toward her or away.

"I'll just refill the wine goblets, my lord, and add them to the table," Jada murmured.

Quiet though the manservant's voice was, it was a shattering intrusion. Lily jerked away from his touch, slapped the book shut and slammed it down on the pile. Her hands were trembling.

After sucking in a deep breath to compose himself, Wulf clamped down on his temper to avoid snapping at the manservant. "Of course."

Moving neatly around the space, Jada collected the goblets and set them at the table, then refilled them and stepped back. Biting back a smile, Wulf wondered how a dinner conversation with Lily would go. He could hardly wait to find out.

She had backed several steps away and was staring at him as if she half expected him to come after her.

And he was definitely more than half tempted.

But a strategist also knew how to play a long game.

Gesturing toward the table, he said, "Come have a seat. I don't keep an elaborate table during a campaign, but the food will be hot and filling."

"It smells delicious." Her gaze went to the table, and her slender brows drew together. Walking over, she sat at one of the tree-stump chairs before he could move to pull it back for her, then inspected the food on her plate.

Wulf glanced at his plate too. It was piled high with

generous slices of roast venison, potatoes, carrots, and gravy, all perfectly straightforward and easily recognizable, so he wasn't sure what to make of her reaction.

"Like I said, it's not fancy, but I have a good cook, and one of my guard tastes everything before any food or drink is brought into the tent." He sat opposite her and picked up his wine goblet.

As he brought it to his lips, her expression changed.

Jumping up, she slapped the goblet out of his hand. It spun through the air, wine spilling from it in a wide crimson spray like blood spurting from an arterial wound.

He met her wide, frightened gaze. Aggression roared to life in his body, and his thoughts raced like a runaway horse.

They had already drunk from the wine in the jug. When it had been brought into the tent, it had already been tasted. The only way it could have poison in it was...

Before the wine goblet could descend on its inevitable downward arc, Jada moved when he did, whipping out a long knife from a sheath at his waist. As Wulf grabbed his sword from where it lay, the other man kicked the tabletop.

The planks were only loosely laid in place on the wooden frames. Supper dishes, jars of caviar, and chocolate flew everywhere. One plank struck Wulf squarely in the chest, knocking him back a beat, while Lily scrambled away, tripped, and sprawled on the rugs.

Jada leaped.

At Lily.

Wulf gripped his sword by the sheath but he had no time to draw the blade. Growling, he thrust the plank aside and sprang at the other man, body-slamming him.

Agile as a cat, Jada twisted to slice at him with the knife. Jerking up the sword, he blocked the knife from reaching from his throat, but fire ran across the heel of his hand as Jada's blade bit deep.

Lily cried out. Still on the ground, underneath the two men, she had rolled onto her stomach and was trying to crawl away.

Shifting his grip on the sword sheath to use it like a blunt weapon, Wulf slammed the pommel into Jada's face. The man's cheekbone shattered under the force of the blow.

All too often the outcome of a battle was decided not in moments, but in fractions of moments.

A decision to move left instead of right. Weaving when you should have ducked.

Choosing to take a moment to breathe instead of thrusting forward with *everything* you had no matter how loudly your body's instincts screamed at you, no matter how badly you might be wounded.

Jada's battle ended the moment he screamed and fell back. He still fought, still struggled. He might even have believed he was still in the game, but Wulf knew better.

Wulf knew how to push forward no matter what. How to ride that crested wave, because when the battle rage was upon him, it broke everything into those fractions of moments and made them easy to see, and it made him so much faster and stronger than the other guy.

He kept at Jada like a battering ram, striking him again and again. Blood sprayed everywhere from the wound in the heel of his hand and from the wounds splitting open on Jada's contorted features. Wulf's focus had narrowed to a single murderous intent: cracking the other man's skull wide open like an egg.

Trying to protect his face with one forearm, Jada made a wild stab. Wulf caught the other man's wrist and broke it, and the knife fell to the rug.

Cold wind whipped into the tent as the guards sprang inside.

Then a weight landed on his back and slender arms wrapped around his neck from behind.

Lily shouted in his ear, "Wulf, stop it! You're killing him!"

That surprised him so much he actually stopped.

Chapter Five

MUCH LATER, LILY huddled on the pallet in Gordon's tent while she listened to the uproar in the camp.

Wulf and his soldiers were busy for quite some time. As she waited, disjointed images of the evening's events kept flaring in her mind's eye.

The light in Wulf's eyes when he caressed the sensitive skin at her throat.

The single-minded savagery with which the two men had fought. Wulf had transformed into a killer, completely unlike the roguish man who had gently teased a piece of chocolate into her mouth.

That hadn't stopped her from jumping on his back. Almost, she wanted to laugh at the memory of his incredulous expression when he had glared over his shoulder, but a part of her was still in shock, and it was a little too soon for humor. Of all the outlandish things she had experienced in her twenty-seven years, she had never been in the middle of a battle before.

And she had achieved her objective. He had paused long enough for her to tell him, "You aren't going to get any answers if you kill him."

That was when true rationality came back into his gaze. As he straightened from the other man's prone figure, she loosened her hold. Then rough hands grabbed her by the back of the neck and twisted one arm behind her back.

With a snarl, Wulf rounded on the guard who had grabbed her. "Back off! She wasn't attacking me."

Instantly the guard let her go and stammered an apology while others swarmed the manservant. Dangerous, violent psyches buffeted her, along with blasts of severe cold mingling with the heat in the tent. Gordon stormed in, along with Jermaine. They all wanted to fight, but the fight was already over.

Wulf became the calm, cold eye of the storm. The savage killer eased back, and the commander took his place. He rapped out orders, and the manservant was taken away. She shuddered to think of what the rest of that man's life would be like.

It could have gone quickly except she had stopped it. Quick would have been a mercy.

Moving to the edge of the tent, she watched until, suddenly, Wulf appeared in front of her. Someone had tied a piece of cloth around his cut hand.

He gripped her by the upper arms. Urgently he said, "Tell me where you're hurt."

"What? No, I'm not hurt." She blinked at him.

She would have some hefty bruises where they had trampled her before she managed to scramble out of the way, and her ribs ached like a son of a bitch where one of the planks from the tabletop had struck, but that was all. She had done worse damage to herself when she had fallen out of trees as a child.

He moved in close enough his torso brushed against hers. She could feel the heat pouring off him. Despite the crowded tent, she felt so immersed in his presence it was almost as if they were alone.

He ran his fingers over her front, and stroked her cheek. His fingers came away smeared with blood. "You're bleeding somewhere."

She looked down at the crimson splotches on the white cotton material of her shirt, then up into his tight expression and smiled. "That's your blood, not mine. You were flinging it everywhere while you fought."

He gripped her at the juncture where her neck met her shoulder. The firm, heavy weight of his hand pressing down on her made her realize she was shaking. "Don't *ever* jump into the middle of a fight like that again."

"Well, somebody had to stop you." She rubbed her forehead. "You don't know if he's the only one in your camp."

"You could have been injured badly, or even killed." His hard gaze bored into hers.

Were they arguing? She couldn't tell. It had been a hell of a day, she was tired, and the energy that terror had lent to her had begun to drain away. "But I wasn't."

Then his warm baritone sounded in her head. *My*

doctor captured a few drops of wine from the jug. The amount of nightshade in it went far beyond what might have caused the dysentery in my troops. He said a couple of sips would have proved fatal. You saved my life.

He had switched to telepathy, so she did too. *I guess I did.*

She hadn't considered that. As soon as she'd realized the wine had been poisoned, she had reacted. If she had been a calculating person, she could have sat back and watched him drink from his goblet, and then the pesky issue of what to do about the Wolf of Braugne would have vanished.

The role she had played in determining the fate of the poisoner troubled her, but just contemplating the possibility of Wulf's death made her feel physically ill.

And that was extremely disconcerting, to say the least.

He stroked his thumb along her skin, the caress hidden from sight by the fall of her hair. *Thank you.*

Unable to speak, she nodded.

Jermaine appeared at Wulfgar's elbow, his hard expression completely unlike the pleasant man who had helped her on and off the barge. "We're ready."

"Good." Wulfgar's voice turned brisk, although he was slow to release her. "We need to know if he was working with anyone else in the camp and, if so, who they are. I also want to know what caused him to turn traitor. Was he offered money, or did Varian's spies hold something over his head? And when he realized he'd been caught, he didn't attack me—he went for Lily. I want to know if there was a reason for that, and if she might still be in danger."

At that, Lily's breath caught in her throat and she froze, just like a rabbit being hunted by hounds.

As if not moving would do her any good.

Jermaine paused to consider her. "I'll be sure to ask him, but if it came down to a fight between you, he was laughably outmatched. He had to know he couldn't win. He might have hoped to use her as a hostage, because once he'd been caught that was the only way he was going to get out of this alive."

Wulfgar's expression settled into grim lines. "Perhaps that's it, but if something happens to the priestess entrusted to my care, we can kiss any hope of collaboration with the abbey goodbye. We need to be sure." He raised his voice. "Gordon!"

As if by magic, Gordon appeared instantly. "Sir."

"Settle Lily in your quarters and get her some supper. And double the guard outside." Abruptly, he swiveled back to her. "I just disposed of you as though you were a trunk full of books."

It wasn't an apology, but at least it was an acknowledgment. Foolishly, she wanted to smile at him, but she stomped on the impulse. Her impulses and emotions were exasperating, confusing, totally out of control.

She said, "You have a lot going on."

"Yes, and I may be tearing apart the entire

encampment before morning to make sure we've rooted out any further attempts at poisoning." He frowned. "There's a lot to do tomorrow as well. Try to get some rest."

Impulsively, she touched the back of his hand before she could stop herself. "Don't concern yourself with me. I will be perfectly fine. Good night, Commander."

His frown deepened, and he looked as if he might call her to task for calling him that, but one of his guards called for his attention. So after giving her a short nod, he strode out, Jermaine at his heels.

When he left, he took all the remaining warmth with him. Shivering, she tied the fastenings of her jacket together.

Gordon swept off his cloak and settled it across her shoulders. She raised her eyebrows as warmth enfolded her. "That's very considerate. I received the impression you didn't care for me."

As usual, she had blurted out what she was thinking before considering her words, but he didn't appear to take offense. Meeting her gaze, he said, "You saved my commander's life. I don't hate you."

He spoke the truth. As she glanced at his psyche, the enmity from earlier was gone. "Still, you need your cloak, and mine has got to be around somewhere."

"I already located it, and it's not fit to use. It's been splashed with the poisoned wine and trampled underfoot. Come."

He led her out. She barely had a chance to feel the

bite of the cold before he ushered her into a smaller neighboring tent. The interior was very simple. There was a bed pallet piled with blankets and furs, a small trunk, and two braziers that threw off such intense heat she immediately shrugged out of the cloak again and handed it back to him.

"I will be back shortly with another supper," he told her. "Have no fear. Despite recent events, the commander's food is actually guarded quite closely, and I will test your meal myself."

She felt a brief, tired exasperation. He seemed to have forgotten she was the one who had discovered the poisoning attempt earlier. But, unwilling to trample on his newfound chivalry, she said gravely, "Thank you."

He was as good as his word, bringing both supper and another cloak. It was soldier's gear, plain, serviceable, and too big for her. After she had eaten her fill, she wrapped herself up in it and dozed until the upheaval began to subside.

Then weather magic started up again. The cold turned vicious, and when she peeked outside, a driving snow had begun to fall.

She didn't dare linger any longer. The longer she stayed, the more she risked discovery. There would be no better time to do this. Sighing, she sent a silent prayer winging to the goddess.

And Camael responded.

An invisible leviathan moved through the camp. The hairs at the back of Lily's neck rose, and her skin tingled as the goddess's presence poured into the tent. When it passed over her, the light from the braziers darkened, and she looked at everything as if through the gauze of a veil.

Lifting the tent flap, she stepped out. There were guards on her tent, and on Wulfgar's, stationed in front of fires that had been stoked high to help ward off the cold. All were wrapped tightly in double cloaks and stood near a witch who chanted spells in a continuous, hoarse whisper to ward off the weather magic.

Despite the well-lighted area, no one turned as Lily slipped around them and made her way through the busy camp.

A few times soldiers hurried past, and once she had to dodge to avoid one who almost blundered into her, but not one of them looked at her. She slipped past the perimeter sentries and the witch who stood vigil to support them. Heels crunching in the snow, she walked along the curve of the road, back to the town and the docks.

Two guards and a witch stood sentry there as well, uselessly squandering their precious energy to watch the island when nobody who had taken shelter at the abbey would leave without the Chosen's permission. They didn't notice Lily as she walked out on the icy dock.

The night was an immense, dark blue expanse, filled with driving pellets of icy snow that stung the skin, the moon cloaked behind a heavy bank of cloud.

The island itself was a dark, hulking presence, lit

intermittently with bright sparks of light in the windows of the towers, and Lily wanted to be in the comfort and shelter of her own room so badly she could taste it.

She frowned at the large, unwieldy barges. Not only were they frozen in place, it took a couple of people working together to maneuver them.

She said to the goddess, *If you would be so kind, will you help me get home?*

In response to her plea, ice cracked and shifted. She peered into the water, watching as a large shard of ice drifted close and came to a stop beside the dock. It looked to be a larger piece than the rest. Presumably it was strong enough to bear her weight. She sighed.

The goddess murmured, *Remember. Be brave as a lion. Have faith that I am with you.*

The goddess had once said those words to her when Lily had been very young, but faith came so much more easily to a small child who didn't truly understand the dangers in the world.

Gritting her teeth, she gingerly climbed down the slippery ladder and stepped onto the hunk of ice. It bobbed gently in the water, enough to make her breathing hitch, but it held her weight. For a moment, nothing happened.

Then it began to move.

Wrapping her borrowed cloak tighter around her torso, she watched as the island grew near. Following the focus of her intention, the ice took her not to the main dock, but around to the small, private dock that faced seaward.

Carefully she climbed off. Ice coated everything, and it was especially thick where constant waves washed over the stone ledge. It was also ridged and uneven, so even though the soles of her boots were smooth, she was able to gain purchase. Pulling out a large key, she made her way to the iron-bound door, but it, too, was covered in a thick sheet of ice.

How flipping wonderful. She looked around at the splendid isolation of the half-frozen seascape, then up at the cliff that towered over her, and despite the indisputable evidence of the goddess's favor, she felt foolish and very alone.

Pulling her magic together, she sent it out in a raw, inchoate blast of energy that struck the door. It shuddered, and the ice that coated it shattered. Raising more magic, she leaned against the door and strained to sense the heavy bar that she knew was on the other side. After several attempts to shift it with telekinesis, finally she could hear a dull thump as the bar hit the steps.

All but frozen now, she fumbled to insert the key into the solid metal lock. Her fingers had gone numb, and she dropped the key and had to kneel to retrieve it. As she tried again to insert it into the lock, the door jerked open and she tumbled forward in a sprawl.

Grim-faced Defenders filled the stairway inside. Some held torches while others gripped drawn swords. Several steps up, a disheveled Margot and a few other priestesses stood, their Power poised to strike.

Exclamations punctuated the air over Lily's head. Someone lifted her to her feet while others peered outside at the desolate seascape.

"Lily!" Margot shouldered her way down. Briefly, she stared outside too. "How on earth did you get here?!"

"On a p-piece of ice," she said, teeth chattering.

Margot repeated blankly, "You *rode* a piece of ice out to open sea? In a *snowstorm*?"

"Well, I didn't do it all by myself.…" Lily looked around at everyone staring at her, their expressions filled with consternation and awe. "I didn't consider how the door on this side of the island would be frozen shut. I had to knock the ice off before I could try to get it open."

"Several of us felt the blast of Power." After ordering the door to be shut and barred again, Margot grabbed her hands. "Dear goddess, you feel like you've turned to ice yourself. Clear the way!"

Lily let Margot put an arm around her and lead her up the stairs, pausing only to say, "We're so complacent about our impregnability, we've been neglecting to set a watch down here."

Immediately, Margot turned and raised her voice again. "Did you hear her? I want that remedied. If Lily can break in, another witch can too."

"Yes, my lady. I'll post someone down here, around the clock," the captain of the Defenders promised.

As they climbed flights of stairs and strode down hallways, Lily's frozen limbs began to thaw, hazing her mind with exhaustion. Shivering set in.

"Tell me what you need." Margot's arm tightened around her shoulders. "Food? Tea?"

"Nothing right now," she said through clacking teeth. "I just want to warm up and go to bed."

When they reached Lily's quarters, Margot shut the door firmly on the other curious priestesses who had followed them. She marched Lily over to the hearth of a large fireplace where a fire already blazed.

The flames in Camael's own hearth never died. Gratefully, Lily sank onto a pile of large floor pillows, scooting as close as she could to the warmth.

Squatting beside her, Margot grabbed her hands and rubbed them briskly between her own, her mouth set in tight lines. "What drove you to return in such an outlandish manner? Did he mistreat you?"

"No!" she exclaimed. Then she added more quietly, "No, he didn't. He treated me very well, actually. I just... A lot happened, and I have to sort through it all. He was going to send me back this morning anyway, but there was a chance I might be discovered. I wanted to leave before that happened."

"If he found out who you were, he might not have let you go," Margot said acutely. "Okay. Can everything else wait until you've warmed up and gotten some rest?"

"Y-yes, I think so. No, wait." She gripped Margot's hands when the other woman started to pull back. "I don't believe he's responsible for the weather magic, and in any case, no matter who is responsible, we can't stand idly by and let it continue. For one thing, if it isn't stopped, it's going to force him to do something desperate."

"And we may not like what he does next," Margot muttered.

"Right now he's trying to be courteous, but if he's given no other choice, he will take over the town," she said. "He's got to protect his troops. And for another thing, that weather magic is wrong, Margot. It's just wrong. If it continues, it's going to kill people if it hasn't already. And if we let it happen when we have the capability to stop it, we become morally culpable too. I want six teams comprised of our most experienced priestesses and Defenders to go hunting for the sources and to stop them by any means necessary."

Margot's reaction was complex, both fear and satisfaction moving in her green gaze. "I'll confess, it's going to feel good to take action. But if you do that, we lose any semblance of neutrality in what comes next."

Shaking her head, Lily said impatiently, "I've told you before. We never had any hope of remaining neutral anyway."

"War is coming, and we can't stop it," Margot whispered.

"No, we can't," Lily said. "One way or another, Calles is going to fall—either to Guerlan or to Braugne. Our days of remaining an independent principality are over."

Chapter Six

MARGOT'S EXPRESSION TIGHTENED. "How long do you think we have?"

"I don't know. Not long."

"Can you see how it's going to happen?"

"No." She rubbed her tired face. "But it's up to us to see that when we do surrender our autonomy, we do it in a way that creates the best outcome for our people. Camael has been preparing me my whole life to deliver this one message. Every vision and dream she's ever sent me—everything—leads to this."

"I believe you." Margot rubbed her back. "But when we assemble those teams and send them out, the council is going to fight us. It's not that anybody questions your appointment. The whole abbey attended the Choosing ceremony, and Gennita anointed every one of our foreheads with oil—and we all witnessed that magnificent flare of light when the oil touched your skin. But people are people, and this is a massive, frightening change they're facing."

"Well, we're not picking an allegiance yet," Lily said. "We're just taking action because it's the right and lawful thing to do. We need to save lives."

"I agree, but there are going to be consequences. You might not be picking a side yet, but you will, for sure, be making an enemy of whoever is responsible for the weather magic. Not everybody is going to be okay with that."

"Which is exactly why I created the position of prime minister." Turning, Lily laid her head on Margot's shoulder. "You handle the council while I figure out which outcomes are the best for us and what steps we have to take to get there."

"That was our agreement," Margot said wryly.

"So this is your battle to fight, not mine," Lily told her cheerfully. "And we all know how much you love a good fight."

Laughing, Margot hugged her. "I used to think there was nothing more that I wanted in the entire world than to become Camael's Chosen, but now... I don't envy you, Lily."

"Smart woman."

After Margot took her leave, Lily stared into the flames for a long time, hoping beyond hope to gain answers to the questions that plagued her, but the goddess's presence had withdrawn.

Somehow she had to make the choices that would get Calles and the abbey to the right destination. She had to pick one of two men, the wolf or the tiger.

The invading force from Braugne or the neighboring kingdom of Guerlan.

One of them would open the door to a better future. The other one would destroy it.

No matter how Lily strained for clarification, Camael never allowed her to see too far past that one essential choice, but Lily could sense that the right choice would be… somehow better than okay. There was prosperity down that path, even the prospect of happiness.

Whereas the wrong choice would lead Calles into the worst disaster they had ever seen. If they went down that path, many wouldn't survive. Perhaps Ys itself wouldn't survive.

Lily was too new to her position. She'd not yet had the chance to meet Guerlan's King Varian, but Guerlan had always kept peace with Calles and the abbey, and the letters Varian had sent to her were well written. She didn't know if he was kind, or if he had a sense of humor, but he did come across as measured, thoughtful, and fair.

And now she had met the Wolf of Braugne.

Had met him, had liked him, and was drawn to him in ways she had never been drawn to a man before. The rogue who had teased her with such knowledgeable sensuality was all but irresistible.

That very same man was a savage killer who had the soul of a conqueror. But it didn't feel wrong. *He* didn't feel wrong.

She had always thought she would recognize the right man as soon as she had the chance to assess him, but she'd been wrong. Everything she had hoped for when events would reach this moment, everything she had thought she understood, had fallen into disarray.

If Lily were Margot, she wouldn't envy her either.

Finally, her limbs dragging with exhaustion, she went into the bathing chamber to wash. It felt indescribably good to get clean, pull on her oldest, softest nightgown, and crawl into her own bed.

She fell asleep almost as soon as her head hit the pillow and slid into a dream.

A man slipped into her bed and pressed a kiss to her bare shoulder.

Yawning, she complained, *You swore this time you wouldn't be so late.*

I know, I'm sorry. He pulled her back into his arms. *My generals wouldn't stop talking. Let me make it up to you.*

The countryside was at war, and she had turned herself into a gypsy to follow him, but he had made an extra effort to make their private quarters comfortable and inviting, and their nights were filled with peace, passion, and warmth.

His powerful body was nude, like hers, and the muscled length fitting along her back was both enticingly exotic and comfortingly familiar at once. Pleasure, like invisible smoke, unfurled warm tendrils along her nerve endings.

She had to force herself to sound cranky as she replied, *Shh. I'm busy sleeping.*

Are you sure? he whispered huskily in her ear as a long, strong hand curved around the swell of her bare breast. *Are you entirely sure?*

It felt so good when he caressed her, she wanted to arch like a cat underneath his fingers. Instead, she pretend-snapped, *Yes, I'm entirely sure!*

His lips teased the sensitive shell of her ear while clever fingers traced circles on her skin. *I've never known anyone to talk so intelligently in their sleep before. You are a woman of many talents. Now I'm curious to see if you can kiss in your sleep as well.*

When he pulled her onto her back, she pinched her traitorous lips together as they tried to widen into a grin. *You're the most stubborn man I've ever met. Do you always get your way?*

I must confess, I do.

He sounded so smug she burst out laughing, even as she tried to see his shadowed features.

Her body knew his, and her heart had already been given, but for some reason, she didn't know what he looked like, and it was vitally important she see his face.

He lowered his head, and his breath smelled like mint as his warm lips brushed hers. As she threaded her fingers through his hair, he settled his weight more firmly on top of hers and deepened the kiss. His tongue slipped into her mouth.

She plunged awake, heart pounding, and stared dry-eyed at the frescoed ceiling. Centuries ago it had been painted gold and a deep, celestial blue, but at night the brilliant colors were muted.

She could still feel the weight of her dream lover's

body lingering over hers and taste the mint from his mouth on her lips.

When she had created the role of prime minister to the council, she had confessed most of her visions to Margot, but not all of them.

In her earlier visions, there were always two men, and she would fall in love with one of them.

She had met the one who was intent on conquest. She hadn't met the other.

One man, she knew from the visions, would be monstrous, while the other man... Well, the goddess only knew how well he would turn out.

She whispered to the ceiling, "Please Goddess, don't let me fall in love with a monster."

GORDON BURST UNCEREMONIOUSLY into Wulf's tent. "Sir, she isn't there."

For a moment Wulf was convinced he hadn't heard the other man correctly.

He had been awake late into the night and had rested only for a short while before rising again. After Jada had been thoroughly questioned, Wulf had him executed, keeping the whole affair as quick and efficient as possible. Passing judgment and carrying out the sentence was never easy, and he didn't believe in prolonging a condemned prisoner's misery any longer than necessary.

Jada had confessed to having another accomplice, one of the men who worked in the mess tent. That man had to be detained, questioned, and executed too. The second traitor didn't name any more names, but food supply was one of the most critical components of the complex, massive operation of a mobilized army, so Wulf was not content to let it end there. There could have been others that the first two conspirators knew nothing about.

He ordered the witch who had the strongest truthsense to assess statements from every member of the cooking crew while Jermaine's team and the camp doctors searched through the food supplies. All of this had been conducted while the rest of the witches fought to lessen the weather magic's deadly storm to something that was at least survivable.

Now Gordon had put his tent to rights and had served a hot breakfast for two. Dishes piled with meat and potatoes, and mugs of hot tea sat steaming on the reassembled table, waiting for a woman who didn't show.

Wulf had gotten probably an hour's sleep at most, and a dull headache throbbed at the base of his skull.

Rubbing the back of his neck, he snapped, "What did you just say?"

Drawing himself up, Gordon said clearly, "The priestess isn't in my tent. She's gone, sir."

He had surged to his feet before the other man had finished the first sentence. Striding to Gordon's tent, he flung back the flap and glared inside.

The pallet had clearly not been slept in. There was an

impression where it looked like she might have curled up, but the blankets were still neatly tucked in at the edges. The two braziers had gone out some time ago, and the edges of the metal bowls were rimmed with frost. Gordon had left a tall pile of wood just inside near the flap, but it looked like it hadn't been touched.

The evidence kicked Wulf in the teeth. She had not only disappeared, but she had done so some time ago. He lunged around the tent, checking the outside of the walls and along the ground. There were no visible exit points, no signs of struggle. The walls were intact and the fresh fall of snow undisturbed.

Whirling, he glared at Gordon who was on his heels. "There were four guards and a witch out here all night."

"Yes, sir." The manservant's expression was pinched with worry.

Something had gotten past four guards and a witch. Either that something had been Lily herself or it had been whatever had taken her.

"Get the dogs."

"Yes, sir!" Gordon dashed away.

Wulf paced while he waited. Four guards. Four guards and a witch.

What had happened? Had she been frightened? Hurt? There had been no blood, or at least none that he had seen. There could have been small droplets he hadn't noticed, but he didn't want to enter the tent again until the trackers and their dogs had been inside.

Besides, there were other ways of being hurt. He

thought of her slender bone structure, that delicate skin, and her obvious lack of fighting skills, and swore under his breath.

Jermaine had been right about Jada. Lured by the promise of gold, he had turned traitor almost two months ago, and recently he had received a communique to assasinate Wulf before he could reach Guerlan's border.

Lily's presence had been incidental. When Jada had gone after her, he had simply hoped to take a hostage. And the interior of Gordon's tent had not shown any signs of struggle.

Wulf had no reason to believe she had been targeted and attacked. It made more sense that she had left on her own. But he didn't *know* for sure, which left him feeling both angry and...

Not panicked. The Wolf of Braugne didn't panic at mysteries.

But he was riled. Oh yes, he was riled, and he was... most sharply concerned.

Striding back to his own tent, he grabbed his sword and cloak and sent for Jermaine with orders to assemble a team. When the trackers arrived, they moved to the edge of camp and worked with the dogs to get a fix on Lily's scent. Gordon hadn't yet disposed of her cloak, and once the dogs had the scent, the trackers loosed them.

Eagerly they leaped to the hunt, and within moments their simple trajectory became clear. As Wulf and his team followed them down the road, to the docks, his most sharp concern withered on the vine while his anger grew.

When the dogs stopped at the end of the dock, one bayed its frustration.

Wulf knew how the dog felt. Planting his fists on his hips, he glared at the abbey. In the gray, cold morning, the warm golden light glowing from its windows taunted him.

Lily had gotten to the dock, past two—no, three—sets of sentries and witches. She hadn't used any of the barges. No, those barges were too much for one small woman to handle.

So how had she done it? How had she gotten from the mainland dock to that blasted island?

He had no idea, but he was by gods going to ask just as soon as he saw her again. Because he would see her again. He would make damn sure of it.

Tripling the military presence at the wharf, he stalked back to his tent and ate his cold breakfast and drank his cold tea.

He drank her cold mug of tea too while his restless thoughts chewed through possible courses of action.

Last night they had said things to each other. The most important communication had been nonverbal, but the body language she had used had been all too clear. And that conversation wasn't over yet. It had, in fact, barely begun.

She did not get to walk away from him. That was not

THE CHOSEN ✧   83

an acceptable scenario in any hypothetical reality.

She had agreed to be his liaison. She didn't get to back out of that just because she felt like it. *He* would tell *her* when he was done with her. *She* didn't tell him.

His gaze fell on the neat stacks of caviar jars and chocolate bars that had survived the previous night's altercation, along with the strange, ugly can of *Chef Boyardee*.

"Commander!" Lionel threw back the tent flap and stuck his head in. "A large party just launched from the abbey. Two barges, sir."

Wulf grabbed up his cloak and weapons again. "How many?"

"Looks to be around thirty people. The prime minister is one of them. Even at that distance, her red hair is unmistakable."

He buckled on his sword. "Any sign of my priestess?"

He heard how that sounded after the words had left his mouth, and paused, then thought, Hell, yes. She's my priestess, and they'd better give her back.

Lionel shook his head. "They're too far away to tell."

"Thirty people," he repeated grimly. That probably meant several witches, and all of them were going to be better rested and much more highly skilled than any of his. "Muster two hundred troops and cavalry and set up a barricade at the wharf."

"Yes, sir!"

Wulf sent for his horse and resumed pacing. He was

not going to stand on that dock, waiting for her to reappear like some pining lapdog. The Wolf of Braugne didn't panic *or* pine, gods damn it.

When he judged enough time had passed, he mounted his stallion and cantered to the wharf. He had gauged correctly, and the barges were just beginning to dock.

Margot Givegny glared at him from the foremost barge. "You have no right to keep us from moving freely on our own land. Move out of our way, Commander."

Planting one fist on his thigh, he held his restless horse from plunging back and forth and bit out, "If I had a liaison to explain your intentions, I might be persuaded to shift aside and let you go about your business. However, I don't have a liaison any longer. She slipped out of my encampment like a thief in the night."

"She's not your servant," Margot retorted. "She has the right to come and go as she sees fit. None of us are subject to you."

"Well, then." His voice turned silken while he gave her a dark smile. "I don't see how I could let your people pass. After all, without proper representation, how can I be sure you don't mean to attack us?"

Margot's mouth fell open. "For the gods' sake, man, you've got an army of eight thousand troops. What kind of damage do you think we could hope to accomplish against you?"

His smile fell away. Dismounting, he threw the reins to Lionel and strode to the edge of the dock.

"A solitary man tried to poison Lily and me last night. Two men working together have caused illness to run through hundreds of my troops. I count seven women in your party who are not wearing Defender uniforms. That means seven priestesses, who, I assume, are also Powerful witches." He gave her a cold, hard look. "So you tell me just how much damage you could accomplish."

Chapter Seven

THE SPRINKLE OF freckles across Margot's nose and cheeks stood out. As he had spoken, she had paled visibly.

Swallowing hard, she whispered, "Someone tried to poison both of you?"

She was too clearly shaken for it to be an act. His eyes narrowed. It appeared Lily had a lot of explaining to do to more than just him.

He pointed at both barges. "Lily said no one from the island would want to leave as long as we were here. Why are you here? What has changed, and why should I allow you to set foot on land?"

Instantly, she bounded back on form again. Glaring at him, she switched to telepathy. *Keep in mind, Commander—I don't owe you an explanation for anything, and you have no right to prevent us from moving about on our own land, so have a care for how far you push me.*

Even as she scolded, he knew she had switched to telepathy for a reason. Planting his feet wide, he crossed his arms. *And?*

Our Chosen has ordered me to send six teams to hunt down

the weather mages and stop them by any means necessary. A hint of vengeful satisfaction flashed through her narrowed gaze. *So by preventing us from following our orders, you are actually hurting yourself more than anyone.*

He uncrossed his arms. *She agreed to help us.*

No, Commander. Margot shook her head. *We are not offering help to you or affiliating ourselves with anyone. We are only committing to uphold the law and to aid any farmsteads who may be in jeopardy. Our Chosen doesn't want to see innocent people die.*

Bending, he offered his hand. She hesitated for a long moment before she grasped it, and he lifted her unceremoniously onto the dock. "Well, let me help you. I can provide backup to every team."

"No, Commander." Turning, she gestured, and the others disembarked. "We will deal with this on our own."

Frowning, he watched as the teams formed in a line. There was one priestess, or witch, and three Defenders in each team. "Weather mages are Powerful magic users. Going after them will be dangerous work."

"We are well aware of that." Exasperation had entered her voice.

Wulf watched as she walked from team to team, pausing to look into the eyes of each witch. He would have liked to have heard the orders she gave them, but whatever their exchange was, they conducted it in silence.

Waiting until she was through, he said, "At least let us give you horses."

"No, Commander," she said. "Calles will not accept any support from Braugne on this matter, nor will we ask for help from any other principality. The abbey keeps horses at the inns in town. Now, that will be all."

He had to hand it to her. She had only five Defenders that would remain with her, while he had a force of two hundred waiting at his back, yet she still managed to dismiss him as if he were a petitioner or a servant. There was a certain kind of splendid, suicidal arrogance in that.

He could have taken her prisoner. She might have damaged or killed a great many of them before he did, but he could have.

Instead, he relaxed and walked back to Lionel and his mount while the six teams from the abbey slipped through the lines of his troops and made their way to town. Margot and her Defenders climbed back onto the barges and set off for the island.

After watching their retreat across the strait for a few minutes, Lionel rubbed the corner of his mouth. "We could have stopped that."

"Too costly without enough reasonable gain. Besides, I have another idea for how I'm going to deal with the abbey." Mounting his horse, Wulf looked down at Lionel. "Send six bands of our best covert fighters after theirs. I want to make sure they succeed in their mission, whether they want our help or not."

Lionel grinned. "Yes, sir!"

✧   ✧   ✧

AFTER HER DREAM, Lily couldn't fall back to sleep.

She needed to sleep. She had needed quality sleep for months now, but the visions and dreams wouldn't leave her alone, and she never got enough rest.

Finally, even though she still felt desperately tired, she threw herself out of bed, dressed, and tried to tackle at least a few of the never-ending tasks piled on her desk.

There were petitions for the Chosen's personal prayers along with large sums of accompanying donations, requests from other kingdoms and principalities for priestesses in residence, and letters from the Elder Races demesnes on Earth and from Other lands.

There were also over a dozen personal requests and complaints from inhabitants of the abbey, and she had to assess the abbey's finances and either approve or amend the budget for the next quarter year....

Even with the help of a secretary, she felt like she was drowning in paperwork.

How could she approve this budget? Right now the abbey had no business spending money on anything but the most basic of essentials that they needed for survival. They needed to hold on to their gold because they might need to import more food supplies from Earth before they saw any relief from the next harvest.

When Margot brought her a document with the teams she had created, Lily studied the list carefully, then approved it. Immediately after Margot left, a wave of dark emotion washed over her head.

People were going to die. Maybe it would be the weather mages, or it might be people from that list. She knew those people, had eaten meals with them, had laughed at their jokes, commiserated with their challenges, and cheered at their personal victories.

In the cold light of morning, it did no good to tell herself innocent lives were already in jeopardy. That was true. They were, and what was happening was wrong, and the action she had just taken was right, and none of that helped.

For the first time since she had become the Chosen, she had exercised the power of her office in such a way that people would die because of what she ordered them to do.

She whispered to Camael, "Goddess, please be with them."

Sometimes the goddess's presence was bold, vast, and miraculous. Sometimes, all Lily heard was silence. This time she heard silence, but at least the darkness in her heart eased enough for her to turn her attention to other things.

Sitting back in her chair, she opened the drawer that held the packet of letters she had received so far from the king of Guerlan. She pulled them out and read them again.

"… Much as we would like to, we regret that we are unable to attend your ascension ceremony as matters in our own kingdom demand our attention. But we extend many felicitations to you, and in our absence, please accept a gift of toys for the abbey's foundlings, made in your honor since you stand as the finest example in all Ys for how one from low beginnings can achieve great heights. …"

Then the next letter: "… I trust this missive finds your grace well, and you are beginning to find your balance. … I know too well the difficulties in the sudden assumption of an elevated office, especially in the middle of grief, as that is what happened to me when my father died. …"

And from another: "… Summer has once again raced past, and we thank you for the abbey's annual gifts. The wine is especially appreciated. I heard how much you enjoy histories, so I hope you like the books I've sent. I also want to extend a personal invitation for you to attend the Masque here in Guerlan at winter solstice. It is but a week's journey from Calles to the capital, and the city is beautiful during the Masque. Garlands of decorations adorn the streets and shops, and I always host the most lavish gala in the six kingdoms. …"

All told, she held half a dozen missives, each one a polished mix of the official and the personal. Almost certainly the king hadn't written any of them. She had always guessed he had probably dictated the snatches of personal comments, but in truth those, along with the thoughtful gifts, could very well have come from his secretary.

She rubbed her face. Aware of the hard winter they would be facing, she had declined with warm regrets the king's invitation to the Masque.

Now she was second-guessing that decision. If she left right away, she would have enough time to get there by the Masque.

If she could lay eyes on Varian and see for herself what visions there were to see, perhaps she might find the monster she had failed to discover in Wulf.

Or perhaps Varian's psyche would be like his letters, warm and thoughtful, measured and fair.

She wanted to flail. She needed a nap.

What was Wulf thinking today? He had to be so mad at her for abandoning him without a word.

Whether he was angry or not did not bear any relevance in her life. She did not owe him an explanation for anything. As she put the letters away again in their assigned drawer and straightened, Gennita stormed into her office.

"Your grace, I must take a few moments of your time." The older priestess's chin shook.

Lily's shoulders slumped. Even though she had tried to bring kindness and respect to Margot's appointment as prime minister to the council, she had offended Gennita deeply by not offering the position to her. Gennita had been Raella's advisor for decades, and she was the oldest priestess on the council.

Now, no matter how many times she had asked Gennita to keep calling her Lily, Gennita had persisted in the more formal address, and Lily had begun to doubt the break between them would ever be mended.

She said, "Now is not a good time, Gennita."

"This cannot wait!" Gennita advanced into the room. "Your grace, you must rescind the order to send abbey priestesses and Defenders to meddle in affairs that do not concern us!"

The darkness, like grief, threatened to wash over her again, and tension clamped down on Lily so tightly she had to force a deep breath into her lungs. "This affair does concern us. It concerns everyo—"

"Calles is too small to withstand a direct, sustained confrontation with another kingdom! Even now we have the Wolf of Braugne lingering at our door. How do you think that will look to Guerlan—our closest, very large, and very powerful neighbor? You could be jeopardizing generations of peaceful coexistence!"

For a moment she felt like she had in the days directly after her appointment—beset by visions, buffeted by opposition from the more established priestesses in the abbey, and bombarded by the sheer volume of duties that were, apparently, still hers alone to fulfill despite her best efforts to delegate where she could.

She remembered those days all too well, the combination of contradictory forces that competed for her attention and threatened to pull her apart.

Shoving the memories into the past where they belonged, she gritted her teeth and tried for patience. "This is not helpful, Gennita. You are supposed to voice your concerns to the prime minister."

"She won't listen to me!"

Lily's patience fractured. "Margot is doing her job! You must listen to her and do what she tells you to do."

"I can't believe the abbey has come to such a place." Gennita stared at her, betrayal in her gaze. "In the beginning you seemed to have such promise, and I had such high hopes for you. Now, not only are you threatening to destroy our safeguards and traditions, but we stand to lose our allies as well. And you're building walls around you so nobody can urge you to consider a different path. Your grace, you will be the death of Calles if you don't change your ways!"

The words hit Lily's solar plexus as if she had taken a physical blow. Pressing a hand to her stomach, she fought to compose herself.

When she could speak, she said, "Get out."

Gennita hesitated, staring at her as if she expected Lily to change her mind. When Lily said nothing, she turned and left.

For a short exchange, that had been very ugly. Locking her office door, Lily hurried to the winding staircase that led to the Chosen's quarters at the top of the seaward-facing tower. Thankfully she didn't run into anyone.

Once inside, she barred the door, then swiped at the tears that persisted in sliding down her cheeks, still covering her stomach with one flattened hand as if she could protect herself from the emotional blow that had already been struck.

All her life she had done everything she could to ascertain what was best for Calles. She simply couldn't try any harder. To have someone like Gennita, someone who had comforted her when she was small and encouraged her throughout school, say that she might be the death of Calles was incredibly painful.

A brush of cool air touched her hot skin, and footsteps sounded beside her.

"What a shame," Wulf said. "I came all this way to fight with you, but it doesn't look like you're up to it."

The floor slid sideways underneath Lily's feet. Catching herself as she staggered, she whirled to stare at him.

"Are you, Lily?" He advanced. "Or should I say *your grace?*"

He looked ruggedly handsome in a simple white shirt, leather pants, and boots. He also looked harder, meaner, more dangerous than ever, and the normally spacious, elaborately appointed apartment felt much smaller than normal.

The fact that he stood here, in the middle of her tower, was more than outlandish. It was impossible.

"What are you doing here?!" Her gaze flew around. "How in the goddess's name did you get in?"

She caught sight of a pile of foreign objects near one tall window. Even as she darted over to inspect them, Wulf said, "I climbed up and broke a window. I knew it was only a matter of time before the Chosen returned to her tower."

There was a cloak in the pile, along with other woolen wrappings, gloves, and rope, metal tools, and a pair of foot-sized iron frames with spikes at the toes that looked like they could be strapped on over boots. It was climbing equipment.

And there was his sword, sheathed in what appeared to be a shoulder harness, leaning against the wall. He was so confident he wasn't even armed, and somehow that was terrifying.

Or maybe it was mortifying. She wasn't sure which.

She pivoted to face him. He had followed her across the wide expanse of the room and stood with his hands on his hips.

"Are you *insane*?"

He eyed her sardonically, mouth held at a slant. "This from the woman who decided it was a good idea to cross a dangerously icy strait by herself in the middle of a snowy night."

"Oh, I knew what I was doing, and I was just fine!" Feeling the need to flail again, she gestured at the broken window. "But you—*this*—is madness! You could have fallen to your death. What if the Defenders on the walls had seen you? With a couple of well-aimed arrows, they could have killed you! Even now, your body would be dangling out there until somebody cut it down."

"You're not the only one with the ability to cloak her presence." He gave her a narrow smile. "One of my witches threw a cloaking spell over me and a small fishing boat."

Her breath caught. "You said your witches weren't as trained as we are. You trusted your life to that spell?"

"Unlike yours, the one she cast wouldn't have been strong enough to let me through a busy army camp and three sentries, but it was good enough to get me to the seaward side of the island. I moored the boat at the private dock, and climbed a section of your tower that none of the guards on your walls can see."

Her mouth dropped open. The chances he had taken were breathtaking. If the newly posted guards at the bottom of the staircase had heard him, they would be dead right now.

They would, not he. She didn't have a single doubt about it. Her mind tried to gallop down the catastrophic consequences of that, and she had to haul herself back to what was relevant.

Sparing a moment to be grateful for the thickness of the door and the thunderous crash of the sea, she said, "How do you even know about that blind spot?"

"I had an advance scout reconnoiter the island weeks ago." He drew closer, the smooth glide of his body leisurely, predatory. "Back before the snows began. He hired a pleasure yacht and sailed around the island, and afterward he came to the abbey along with a group of petitioners. Apparently visiting the abbey was a pleasant experience. The priestesses he spoke to were very nice, while children played in the courtyards. He drew a map of the weakest points of your surveillance and defense. On this side of the island, you rely too much on the elements to protect you."

She had said almost that very thing the night before, but it felt devastating to hear Wulf state it so coldly. "You scouted us weeks ago."

"I have been scouting the seat of every principality. Like you said, *your grace*—I'm always plotting four steps ahead."

She had been right. He was still very angry. Retreating a step, she asked, "When did you discover who I was? Did that manservant tell you when you questioned him?"

"I knew almost immediately."

She felt again as if the floor tilted sharply on her. "You knew?"

"I guessed when we first met on the dock. Everyone else in your party acted their part. They focused on me and on your minister, but you were off script. You weren't paying attention to us—you were focused on other things, and you didn't stay in formation. Instead, you maneuvered around a little as you assessed us. And of all the Defenders on that dock, the strongest ones had been stationed at your back, not your minister's. And when you agreed to come with me, everyone reacted."

Intensely chagrined, she closed her eyes. Even at the time, she'd had no doubt he noticed everything. Apparently she seemed destined to make accurate enough observations, but she was a spectacular failure at extrapolating anything useful from them.

"I had no idea Margot had arranged the Defenders

like that," she whispered. "So when you picked me out of the crowd, you already knew."

"I suspected, but I didn't know for sure until you told me about the bicycles." He shook his head. "Nobody talks more lovingly than themselves about their own pet projects, and you loved bringing that opportunity to the town. Your face lit up when you told me about it. After that, I thought once or twice you might confess. Remember when I said your minister didn't have any objection to giving me a priestess, she just didn't want it to be you? I thought you were going to tell me then, but you didn't. You managed to slide away from it."

He had known all that time. Instead of confronting her, he had watched and waited, conversed and assessed. And she hadn't suspected, not even once.

With Gennita's bitter words still twisting like a knife in her gut, he couldn't have confronted her at a worse time.

What else had she missed? What else, what else?

The visions were always strongest when she felt the most broken and vulnerable, as if those were the times when divinity could truly shine its light into her mind. Now they swept over her again, blinding her to the physical world around her.

Bitter winter, lean harvest. Kingdoms filled with unrest. A darkening over the land, clashing swords, and two men in mortal combat. One of them would grind Ys to dust.

And always the fall of Calles...

You will be the death of Calles if you don't change your ways!

While she observed so much, she failed to really see.... And people would die on her word, by her actions.

Would she be responsible for the fall of Calles? Again, she felt a tearing sensation, as if contradictory forces would pull her apart. Even though she tried to repress it, a low groan escaped, and she bent at the waist.

Goddess, I can't do this.

"Lily," Wulf said. "What's wrong?"

Dimly, she was aware that the hateful sardonic tone had vanished, but still, his presence was all but unbearable. She felt too raw, too wounded.

"Don't look at me," she gritted while her tears dropped onto the marble floor. "You invaded my private space just because you got mad. You don't get to see this. This is *mine*, do you hear? Mine to deal with, not yours."

Silence throbbed to the beat of the blood pounding in her face. Still bent over, she focused on the floor underneath her feet, on taking her next breath.

She was excruciatingly aware of the moment when he shifted. Out of the corner of her eye, she saw his blurred figure squat beside her. He had angled his face away.

"I'm not looking at you." His words were quiet and even. Nonaggressive. "You abbey women are fierce about your boundaries, aren't you?"

She coughed. It was not quite a laugh. "Damn right we are. Defending boundaries is every bit a tenet of our faith as nurturing those at our hearth and practicing the healing arts."

Still not looking, he reached toward her. His fingers ran lightly up her thigh to her waist, searching her body by touch until he found her forearm and curled his fingers around it. Slowly he tightened his grip, applying pressure until that became the focal point, not the tumultuous crash of thoughts, emotions and images roiling in her mind.

Like the tide as it ebbed, the visions receded. No longer feeling quite so crushed, she took a deep breath, then another, and the tears stopped. Scrubbing the wetness from her face, she straightened.

He stood when she did. Instead of releasing her, he ran his hand down her arm to clasp her fingers lightly. "That has got to be the most unsatisfactory argument I've ever had."

She almost laughed again, but damn it, no, she wouldn't. "For what it's worth, I really don't think you realize how *crazy* it is that you climbed my tower."

"Well, for what it's worth, the blind spots my scout mapped are useless for anything other than a small, targeted strike force. You might get an assassin up here, but not a full-scale invasion."

She said dryly, "A danger no Chosen in the past several *hundreds of years* has faced."

He shrugged. "Fix metal bars at the windows and

you'll be safe enough." Pausing to scoop up a leather bag, he led her to the array of floor pillows in front of the fireplace. "And lady, you don't have any high ground from which to call *me* crazy."

When they reached the pillows, he tugged her down.

She shouldn't sit with him. She should do something else, like take advantage of his relaxed demeanor to pull away from his hold, run for the door, throw off the bar, and scream for help. She had seen for herself just how fast he was, but he was already half sitting. She might get away with it.

But she was tired, and that sounded like so much more hassle than she wanted to face. The consternation, the alarm, the certain violence.

He couldn't escape out the tower without being killed, so he would have to take her hostage. The whole abbey would be thrown into an uproar, and she and Wulf would have to go out into the cold again, and she'd only just gotten back.

Was it wrong of her to want to just sit? It didn't feel wrong. She glanced at his psyche where the shadow of a wolf lay on its paws, its entire attention focused on her. The wolf was beautiful. It was a dangerous, perfectly natural creature. She kept hunting for the monster in him, but the monster wasn't there.

Heaving a sigh, she gave up, sat beside him, and curled her legs underneath her. "What are you doing?"

"I brought your presents." Opening the bag, he pulled out the chocolate bars and the can of Chef

Boyardee along with the jars of caviar and salt bread. "I also brought supplies for myself. Climbing in cold weather is hungry work."

He had brought presents to a fight. Oh goddess. What did she feel? Exasperation? Laughter? What? Throwing her arms wide, she flung herself back onto the pillows. "It's going to be dark soon. You need to go, Wulf."

He cocked an eyebrow. "Oh, I can't go out in that. If I try to make that climb in the dark, it'd kill me. I'm going to have to stay until morning."

He was lying, shamelessly. He had to know she could sense it.

She squinted at his face, which remained in profile. He still hadn't looked at her. How strange, that such an ephemeral boundary would hold him when he had trampled over almost everything else. There was a sophisticated reasoning behind it that she couldn't quite grasp.

"You know I can tell you're lying, don't you?" she demanded.

The corner of his lips pulled into a smile. "You've already proven you don't want to hurt me, so we'll have to find a way to coexist for a while."

She glared at him. "Have you made a plan for how your witch is going to cloak you when you go?"

He shrugged. "I thought I might know someone who would agree to help me out."

He was impossible. She couldn't throw him out the

window. She wouldn't call for help. If he tried to leave during daylight, he would almost certainly be seen unless she cloaked him. And if she didn't agree to help him, he would be stuck in her tower until the next night.

Of course she would help him. She couldn't stand idly by and watch him get killed, and he knew it. Besides, it might be the only way she could get rid of him.

As she debated, he said gently, "Put it all aside for now. Take a break from whatever demons are crushing you. What was your final verdict on the caviar? Yes or no?"

Pinching the bridge of her nose, she said, "No."

"Great. All the more for me." He set the caviar aside. "Now, about this Chef Boyardee. You are going to owe me for this."

"What do you mean?" She snorted. "I don't owe you anything."

His smile deepened. Reaching behind him, he dangled the can in her general direction. "What is the verdict? Do you want this? Yes or no?"

Damn it, she did. She hadn't eaten much since the late supper Gordon had brought to her tent, and she was hungry. "Yes."

"Then you owe me the story of how you came to like this food from Earth, and why." He paused. "You also owe me a taste so I can see what all the fuss is about."

Okay, he finally got her. Curling on her side, she laughed. "You are going to hate it. Everybody does. It's horrible. Objectively, even I know that. It shouldn't even be called food."

"Now I'm even more intrigued to hear your story." Using a knife, he opened the can by puncturing the edges of the lid repeatedly until he could bend back the metal. Cautiously, he inspected the orange contents and sniffed at it.

Laughing harder, she sat and held out her hand. "Here, give it to me. And stop trying so hard to avoid looking at me. It's all right now." She added quickly, "But it's still not all right that you're here."

"I am well aware of that, Lily." Turning his head, he looked into her eyes and smiled. "Yet here we sit. I propose we make the best of it."

Chapter Eight

H~E WAS SUPPOSED~ to be brutal and domineering, not charming and insouciant. Now he really wasn't living up to his reputation.

The intensity in his gaze was too much. She reached for his knife, and he let her take it. "This is supposed to be heated, but I like it cold too."

Using the tip of his knife, she fished out a piece of ravioli and ate it with relish while he watched her, still smiling.

When she swallowed, he rubbed the corner of her mouth gently with the ball of his thumb, then licked it.

Dear goddess. Warmth washed over her skin.

He smiled. "Tell me the story."

She surveyed the contents in the can. "I'm not actually from Ys. I used to live in a place called southern Indiana."

He puzzled over that information, then said, "The language on the can is English."

"Yes. Indiana is in the United States, in North America."

Opening a jar of caviar and a packet of salt bread, he

dipped a corner of a wafer in the jar and then popped it in his mouth. Around the bite, he said, "You must have had quite a journey. Ys doesn't have any crossover passageways to America."

"No, all our passageways are connected to Europe." She looked into the cheery flames leaping in the fireplace. How could she tell this story quickly? "My early childhood was... complicated. When I was a toddler, we were poor, and we lived in a small town. My mother drank, and she had several men come and go until one of them stayed. He cooked meth, which is a very addictive, illegal drug."

As she spoke, his subtle playful attitude had disappeared, and he watched her intently. "That doesn't sound like a good home for a child."

"No," she said. "Mind you, I was too young to comprehend most of it. When the abbey took me in, the priestesses scried to find out where I was from and what had happened to me. I'm sure I breathed chemicals I shouldn't have, and I was mostly left to my own devices, but I didn't really understand, you know? I do remember that one of my favorite meals was Chef Boyardee and a packet of M&M's—which is a kind of chocolate candy— for dessert. Occasionally I still like to eat them."

He tucked a strand of hair behind her ear. "How did you get from there to here?"

She blew out a breath. "Camael led me here. I was a strange child, and... Let's just say I saw things that weren't physically present. I still do."

He frowned. "Didn't your mother ever have you tested for magic?"

She said wryly, "I don't think she was that functional. Anyway, one night a shining woman walked into my bedroom. She kissed me on the forehead and said, 'Come with me, little love.' She was so beautiful, and I was very excited, and I asked if she would be my new mommy. She told me, 'In a way, I will. But you must be brave as a lion and do as I say.' So I did. I took my pillow and my stuffed bunny, and I walked out of the house."

"How old were you?" He took the can from her, scooped out a ravioli, and ate it.

Laughing at the face he made, she replied, "I was three. Outside, the shiny woman disappeared, but I could hear her voice, and I could feel when she nudged me. Our house sat at the edge of town, and she led me into the forest, past the ruins of a building, and along a creek—and as I walked, everything around me changed. Suddenly it was daylight, and I was in a field, and there was no creek, nor were there any ruins. I had walked down a crossover passageway."

At this point in the story, his gaze never left her face. "Were you frightened?"

Shrugging, she told him, "Sure, a couple of times. But at first I was too excited to get to my new home and mommy. Then I was bored. After that I got used to it, I guess. When I was found, apparently I'd been wandering the countryside for more than a month."

"This story is killing me. You were three?" He shook his head. "It's a miracle you survived. What did you eat?"

She took the can back from him. "I ate the mushrooms and the berries the goddess told me to eat and drank at streams when she told me to drink. I had my bunny and my pillow, and I slept in the woods."

He blew out a breath. "Nobody can survive on berries and mushrooms for a month, especially not a small growing child."

She laughed. "I know, right? They told me I was in remarkable shape for everything I'd been through—my teeth were perfect, and I was healthy, and fit, and very, very dirty."

"In Ys."

"Yes, in Ys." Scraping the sides of the can, she carefully licked the sauce off the blade. "Since discovering a new crossover passageway is officially a very big deal, Raella sent priestesses to verify everything in person. They interviewed everyone in the town and searched for ten miles in every direction." She paused. "They found the creek and the ruins—they learned it had once been a courthouse—but there was no passageway. The house where I'd lived had burned to the ground early one morning. The fire had killed my mother and her boyfriend in their sleep, but they never discovered the body of a child. That's all I know. The abbey took me in, and I've been here ever since."

Setting the empty can aside, she avoided looking at him. While the consternation and awe she saw at times in other people's faces was understandable, it also made her feel lonely and isolated. She didn't want to see that in his expression.

Long, lean fingers came under her chin, and he coaxed her around to face him. Feeling cranky, she complied. Fine. How he felt about her was irrelevant anyway.

What she saw in his gaze melted away her crankiness. His eyes were alight with... admiration? Respect? "I am beyond honored to meet that brave little girl."

That was a stupid thing to say. She had no business feeling touched by it or warmed in any way. "That little girl has been gone for twenty-four years."

"Of course she's not gone. She still lives inside you, and you have her magic and her bravery." He caressed her cheek. "My advance scout reported that, while he was here, he heard people talking of the new Chosen. They said she was kind and thoughtful and a true visionary in every sense of the word. Your people love you."

Despite the harsh words she and Gennita had exchanged, she knew it was true. Her people did love her. The ones she had sent out to fight and die loved her. Wulf's face disappeared in a blur.

He said, "Don't let those demons back in, Lily."

She had to push her lips together hard before she could whisper, "I sent people out to fight today. I sent friends out to fight today, and some of them won't come back."

A long silence greeted those words. "Was this your first time?"

Nodding, she swiped at the tears that spilled over. "Like I said—this is mine to deal with. But today was a hard day."

Cupping the back of her neck, he kissed her forehead. His lips were warm and firm. "In case you were wondering, no, it doesn't get easier. You'll need to find ways to cope with it."

"I know. And I need to find ways to better handle opposition and conflict. I had a bad run-in with one of the elders on the council earlier. I don't think our relationship is ever going to be the same."

He murmured as if to himself, "You're not going to let me ride in and fix all your problems, are you?"

With a snap of focus, she met his gaze. "What do you think?"

He chuckled. "I think I just came up against one of those boundaries again." Sobering, he continued. "I might not be able to fix your problems, but I've been in command for a lot longer than you. If I might offer a small piece of advice, don't be too nice tomorrow. Discourse and disagreement are one thing, but don't let anyone challenge your authority or show you disrespect. You're the one in charge, not them."

She groaned and clapped her hands over her face. "She was one of my teachers. I used to sit on her lap for story time."

"Poor Lily." He rubbed her back. "Do you still need

to sit on her lap for story time?"

"What?" She straightened and glared at him. "No!"

✧ ✧ ✧

WULF LOVED WATCHING how her gaze sparked, so much so that he was tempted to needle her further. But behind that flash of fire, there was real exhaustion, and dark smudges circled her eyes.

Instead, he shrugged. "Sounds like you know things have moved on. While you haven't told me what you two said to each other, maybe she needs to be reminded of that too."

The corners of her mouth turned down. "I'll think it over."

"Good." He was still hungry. Now that she no longer needed his knife to eat the appalling orange food, he spread more caviar on salt bread and ate. "Don't mind me. Go ahead and help yourself to the chocolate."

While he braced for another argument, this time she surprised him and reached for the candy. "You have destroyed my integrity. I won't forget this."

He nudged her shoulder with his. "No one need ever know about the chocolate and that other weird orange stuff. Your secret is safe with me."

Giving him a lopsided smile, she broke a chocolate bar into pieces. "We've talked more than enough about me. What about you? What was your childhood like?"

"Mine was as straight and uncomplicated as an arrow. Nothing cutthroat, no funny business, no disappearing crossover passageways. I roamed a little too far sometimes, I was cosseted by everyone, and my curfew was my stomach. I was always home by supper."

"Your mother was lady of Braugne, correct?"

"That's right." When he finished the caviar, he ate the last of the salt wafers, then looked around with regret. He was still hungry. "Her first husband died after she had Kris. After a few years, she remarried and gave birth to me. I was always thrilled that he was the heir. There was no way in hell I wanted to rule Braugne."

He still didn't. Now he wanted to rule all of Ys.

She hesitated, then said, "You're so sure Varian had your brother killed… Do you have proof?"

Instead of answering right away, he leaned back on one elbow as he regarded her. Scooting around, she turned to face him and leaned on her side too, propping her head on the heel of one hand.

The glow of the firelight gilded her skin with gold. At first he hadn't noticed her in the group on the dock. All his attention had been on her pretty, fiery prime minister.

Then, gradually, Lily had captured more and more of his attention, until now he couldn't look away from her.

He couldn't believe how beautiful she was, and how sophisticated the subtle play of her expressions were. And he couldn't stop touching her.

Capturing her hand, he played with her fingers. "Braugne has always been a cash-poor kingdom. Our country is mountainous, splendid, and unforgiving. We can feed and house our own, and our goats and sheep are some of the hardiest stock a farmer could ever hope to have, but to date, our biggest exports have been iron, a little copper, and salt from mining."

She played with his fingers too. It was such a small intimacy, but her touch sent a trail of liquid fire running through his veins.

"That's about the extent of what I know about Braugne," she admitted.

"We also have no access to the advantages that crossover passageways can give to a kingdom. Neither do Karre or Mignez. Those advantages have been largely enjoyed by Guerlan, Calles, and Chivres. Not only are those passageways further out of reach for the rest of us, most of them levy taxes on the usage of them."

A frown creased her forehead. "I never considered that inequity before. Sometime I would like to discuss ways we might change that."

Bless her. He almost kissed her.

He intended to change that too, to level some of the inequities in the richer kingdoms while bringing more opportunities to the poorest. She had been right. He had the soul of a conqueror and the drive to see the conquest through.

But he was unwilling to steer things in that direction, and he didn't want to rile her. He wanted more of this calm, private conversation.

So for now he compromised and pressed her fingers to his lips. "I would like that. But to get back to your question, last year Varian approached my brother. He offered a treaty to lease several thousand hectares of land to Guerlan for a hundred years. Varian's envoy said it was for hunting purposes. His king was eager to explore the vast and magnificent challenge of hunting the wild boars, mountain lions, and firedrakes in Braugne."

Her eyebrows rose as she considered that. "Are firedrakes difficult to kill?"

"Extremely. Their bodies are about the size of a large mastiff, not counting their tails, and they have teeth almost as long as the length of my hand."

She eyed him curiously. "Do they really spit fire?"

"It burns like fire, but it's more like an acid that will eat your flesh from the bone if you let them spray you. They're also smart like feral cats, and very fast, so hunting them is not a safe pursuit, yet apparently Varian was eager to try it. Kris told him he would take the winter to consider the proposal. Signing a hundred-year lease wasn't something to do lightly. Plus it bothered him. Why a hundred years? Varian's in his midthirties. By the time forty or fifty more years have passed, he won't be hunting anything. Still, the money was tempting. There was a lot we could do with it."

She muttered, "I'm waiting for the story to turn bad."

He squeezed her hand. "Events transpired over some time, but the story does turn pretty quickly. Kris thought about the treaty while Varian's envoy wintered at our court. He was funny and charming and persuasive, and yet why the hundred years? Why that tract of land? The only thing it had ever been good for was a salt mine that everybody knew was almost played out. So Kris set me to the task of finding out why."

"And did you?"

Wulf thought back over the long, painstaking investigation. Having the Guerlan envoy followed, intercepting messages, uncovering, bit by bit, a network of Guerlan spies that had insinuated itself into the kingdom, and the slow build of incredulous anger at what he discovered.

"It took me and my team of investigators several months, but I did," he told her. "Over the past decade, Varian has quietly developed a presence in our mining towns, and he's been spying on our explorations. It turns out the mine on the land he wanted to rent was almost played out for salt, which everyone had already known. But the real news was, the miners had struck gold instead."

Chapter Nine

S HE STRAIGHTENED. "AND you didn't know."

"Correct. Varian bribed the mine operator, who was reporting to him. The miner who made the actual discovery had died in a fall, his death ruled an accident, and the town was already half abandoned as people were leaving to seek out opportunities in other places. If Kris had signed that lease, all the proceeds from the mine would have been Guerlan's for a hundred years."

Outrage flashed across her face. "What happened next?"

"Kris lost his temper." Wulf sat up too and crossed his arms over upraised knees. "I'd been in command of his army for several years, but he insisted on leading a force himself to confront the mine operator. My job was to finish rooting out all the other Guerlan spies in our mining operations. He headed out just before midsummer. That was the last time I saw him alive, or any of the troops that went with him. We've recovered most of the bodies, but we haven't found Kris's yet."

She touched his hand. "I can hear how much you loved your brother by the way you talk about him. Do you know what caused the avalanche?"

"We found residues of oil, and my witches say there was some kind of magic compounded with it. And I have a heavy weight of evidence that proves Varian's been spying on Braugne for years and conspiring to steal our resources." Tightening his hands into fists, he added between clenched teeth, "So yes, I have more than enough to justify marching on Guerlan, and I plan on ramming the evidence down Varian's throat when I get there."

"I see." She started to say something else but was interrupted by a knock on her door. She froze and stared at him.

The knock sounded again, and she jumped.

After tensing, Wulf relaxed again and spread his hands. He had taken the risk in coming, and now he had to go with it. He had to trust her.

"You need to answer that," he told her. "If you don't, they'll panic and break down your door."

As if he had lit a fire under her, she jumped to her feet. "Just a moment—I'm coming!" she shouted. She glanced at the chocolate wrappers, the can, and the empty jars strewn on the floor and threw up her hands. Then she whirled to look at his equipment by the wall. Pointing to an open doorway, she hissed, "Quick—grab your stuff and go into my bedroom!"

Even as he sprang into action, he bit back a smile. Yes, it might have been a risk, but he had known he could rely on her. Scooping up his things, he loped through the doorway into a darkened room, glided quietly to a stop against one wall, and listened.

Wood scraped as she unbarred and opened the door. "What is it, Margot?"

Ah, the Chosen's ever-annoying prime minister. Wulf rubbed his chin with the back of one hand. She was quite the perpetual asshole, that one.

"You didn't come down for supper, so I wanted to check on you, to see if you're all right," Margot said. "Honey, have you been crying?"

"Yes," Lily said. "And no, I don't want to talk about it right now."

"Are you sure? I'm here if you need me."

"I know you are." Lily's voice warmed. "And that means a lot to me. Right now I just need to be by myself. It's hard to wait, you know?"

"I do know." Margot's own voice was somber. "Can I at least send someone up with a supper tray?"

"Not tonight. I ate some snacks, so I'm not hungry." She said firmly, "Thank you for checking on me. I'll see you in the morning."

"All right." When he didn't hear the sound of the door closing right away, he could sense that Margot lingered, reluctant to leave. "Good night, Lily. Try to get some sleep."

"You too."

There was a rustle of clothing, then, finally, the sound of the door latching followed by the thump of the bar dropping into place.

When Wulf strolled out, he found Lily leaning against the door with her forehead pressed to it, shoulders slumped. She looked so dejected, he set his equipment to one side, strode over, and pulled her into his arms.

Margot was not the only perpetual asshole. He was one too.

He had come all this way to fight with Lily, but he had come for other reasons too. He wanted to finish that conversation they had started back in his tent. He had been intent on seduction because *she* didn't get to leave him. He'd leave her when he was done with her.

Only now he couldn't. He recognized all the cues that told him if he pushed, he might still have her for the night. After first stiffening, she turned into his hold and rested her head on his shoulder, and the trust in that gesture tied him more irrevocably than any of her invisible boundaries.

If he pushed her now, she might succumb, but her heart and mind were so weighed by other matters he might also lose her afterward, and if he did lose her, it would only be what he deserved. Besides, he didn't want to be that kind of selfish man.

He said into her hair, "I can't solve all your problems. I can't make it better. I couldn't save that mining town. I couldn't protect my brother, and I don't want to stop what I intend to do next. But if you'll let me, I can hold you for a little while. I would very much like to do that."

Slowly her arms stole around his waist. He was ferociously glad of that, and proud of how she leaned against him now, and determined to be worthy of it.

She whispered, "I would like that too."

Walking her back to the sitting area, he coaxed her onto the couch, and when she sat beside him, he pulled her into his arms again. Tentatively, they explored this strange new definition, her slender body fitting against his much longer frame, her head resting on his shoulder, his cheek resting against the top of her head.

As they settled, something happened to Wulf, something he hadn't seen coming. For so long, he had carried a hard, cold knot of rage in his chest. He had grown so used to living with it, he only just became aware of its existence again as it warmed and eased into something that felt remarkably like comfort.

Damn it. He had meant to comfort her. Turned out, she was comforting him. He remembered the sick drop in his gut when he realized Kris had died, thought of his brother's missing body, and his eyes grew damp.

Tightening his arms, he held her and they watched the bright flames in the fireplace. After a while, he realized there wasn't any stacked wood nearby. Neither of them had done anything to fuel the fire, yet it crackled as if it had been newly started, and the logs still looked quite fresh.

It was just one of the many miracles that hovered about Lily like fireflies glowing in the dark, and for the first time in his life, Wulf prayed.

I want her, he said to Camael as he stared fiercely into the flames. *In fact, I want her more than anything I've ever wanted in my life. She might be your Chosen, but you'd better be prepared to share.*

So it wasn't the most supplicant or reverent prayer ever said, and Wulf wasn't the pilgrim type. He was who he was.

The goddess didn't answer.

Of course she didn't. Gods didn't talk to him.

But a bolt of lightning didn't strike him dead either. After a long moment of listening to the peaceful quiet, interrupted only by the snap and crackle of the flames, he counted that as a win.

Lily stirred. "How long do you think we'll have to wait before we hear anything?"

"There's no way to know, love. We'll hear when we hear." He pressed his lips to her forehead as he debated. Then he said, "If it helps you to know this, I sent my best covert warriors after yours with orders to assist if your people needed it."

When her shoulders started to shake, he felt a brief alarm until he realized she was laughing. "Why am I even surprised?" she said. "Of course you did. Do you always get your way?"

He tilted his head as he considered that. "I must confess I do."

She bolted upright and stared at him, eyes wide.

"Surely by now that wasn't a surprise?" he said, baffled by her reaction.

"No." She gave him a soft, strange smile. "I guess it wasn't."

He touched her cheek. "I want to stay, but I'd better go. You need real rest, and this is not where I'm supposed to be."

"That's the most sensible decision you've made all evening." She looked worried. "Are you sure you'll be able to make that climb and travel across the strait again at night?"

He rolled his eyes. "Don't you even go there."

She started to laugh again. "Very well, forget about crossing the strait at night—are you sure you'll be able to make that climb in the dark?"

"I left the pitons in place. Getting down will be a lot easier than getting up." He started to smile. "Why, are you concerned about me?"

"Maybe… a little." She followed him as he gathered up his equipment and strode over to the broken window. "Maybe I don't want to look out my window in the morning and find your broken body dangling at the end of a rope."

"Don't worry. I will be cold but fine." He paused. Her eyes were rimmed with red, and one cheek bore a crease from his shirt. Setting everything aside, he cupped her face with both hands and kissed her.

Those delicate, soft lips were another miracle. She kissed him back, and that was a miracle too.

He whispered against her mouth, "After I get justice for my brother, I am going to take control of Ys and make it a better place. I already have treaties with Karre and Mignez. Just so we're clear."

When he lifted his head again, she stared at him warily. "I see?"

She sounded so mystified, he had to kiss her again.

He could have told her, "I'm going to take you too, and keep you for my own."

He could have, but he didn't. Some conquests needed to be made in careful, strategic steps.

"Get some sleep, love," he said. "We'll talk again soon."

AFTER SHE HAD thrown a cloaking spell over him and he had climbed out the window, Lily went to bed.

Much to her surprise, she did sleep soundly for a few hours, but then restlessness set in before dawn. Driven by tension that knotted her body, she rose, washed and dressed for the day, and left her tower.

Down in the kitchens, they had barely started to cook, but when she appeared, the head cook was honored to fix an early breakfast of scrambled eggs, buttered bread, and sweet, hot tea for her.

After she ate, the restlessness was worse. She went up to her office, started a fire, and answered a few letters. When her secretary, Prem, appeared, she smiled and said, "Good morning. Please bring Gennita to me at once."

"Yes, your grace." Prem smiled back and whisked away.

The minutes advanced so slowly she could almost hear the wheels of time grinding together. She was all but leaping out of her skin. Her heart raced, and a fine film of sweat covered the back of her neck.

What was wrong with her? She wasn't looking forward to the upcoming meeting, but she didn't feel bad enough to warrant this physical reaction. She forced herself to answer another letter.

When Gennita finally appeared in her doorway accompanied by Prem, Lily told her secretary, "That will be all for now." To the older priestess, she beckoned. "Please step inside, and if you would be so kind, shut the door behind you."

"Certainly, your grace." Gennita gave her a forced smile. After closing the door, she turned and said, "I expect this is about what we discussed yesterday."

Lily remained seated. "We didn't have a discussion," she said. "We had an argument. You were inappropriate, and you made accusations."

Accusations that were very hurtful. But no. Don't talk about feelings.

The older woman stiffened. "You *grace*, I don't appreciate being scolded as if I were a misbehaving schoolgirl."

"Neither do I." Lily paused to let her cold words sink in. "Out of the love and respect I have for you, I am going to give you a choice, Gennita. There is a wonderful appointment in Karre, just waiting for the right priestess and her family. It's clear they value the work that

Camael's priestesses do. You have the right healing skills they need. They have a large, comfortable house with gardens that sound beautiful—your husband would love them—and the temple is well kept. And the stipend sounds very reasonable. You could have a happy life there if you want."

As she spoke, tears started in the other woman's eyes and she looked shaken. "We've lived here for the past twenty years. My grandchildren are here. Are you ordering me to go to Karre and leave behind the rest of my family?"

"No," Lily told her firmly. "I am offering you a choice, and you have a day to make it. You can explore this new opportunity in Karre, or you can stay here. But if you stay, you must abide by the new rules I've set in place. There's a time for discussion, and there's a right way to disagree. Confronting me in my office, ignoring me when I tell you to stop, and hurling emotional accusations at me is never going to be acceptable. Do I make myself clear?"

"Yes, your grace," Gennita whispered.

The older woman looked so miserable, Lily pushed away from her desk and walked around to her. Taking Gennita's hands, she pressed them and said quietly, "Life feels scary right now. The abbey may thrive or fail on choices that I have to make, and if you think I'm not aware of that every moment of every single day, you are badly mistaken. But you must remember—the goddess picked me, and I still have to make those choices to the very best of my ability."

"I know the position is hard." Gennita's voice was choked. "Raella had sleepless nights over some of the things she had to do."

Lily took in a deep breath. "I'm sure it doesn't help that I don't see things the same way you do. I don't put information together in the same way as you, and I understand that must be frightening and inexplicable at times. If you feel like you must go, I will miss you. But if you stay and do something again like you did yesterday, I will make the next appointment a mandatory one."

"I understand."

Lily turned back to her desk, picked up the appointment request from Karre and handed it to the other woman. "Why don't you read the details of the request over with your husband? Let me know by noon tomorrow if you want to take the position."

Beginning to look calmer, Gennita accepted the letter. "Thank you, Lily. I can see the care and attention that you put into picking this opportunity. You even thought of Edward's love of gardening. And I apologize for yesterday. I didn't consider my words very well."

Lily said, "Apology accepted. Now, if you'll excuse me, as you can see my desk is worse than ever."

"Of course." Gennita paused, glanced at Lily's desk, then gave her a tentative smile. "If I might make a small suggestion?"

Lily reached for more patience. "What's that?"

"Get a second secretary. Prem is wonderful, but I

don't think she's up to handling some of the more challenging tasks that you could still delegate to someone else. Dulcinda, perhaps, or maybe Evie." Gennita met her gaze. "You're right—life feels a little scary right now. You should be free to focus on those bigger decisions, not paperwork."

Lily blinked. "Thank you. I'm going to seriously consider that."

After Gennita had gone, she turned in a circle and stared at the empty room. While Gennita had been predictably upset at being given an ultimatum, the conversation hadn't gone as badly as it could have.

It had actually gone better than she'd expected. Gennita had even called her by name again.

But instead of feeling relieved, she felt worse than ever. Her hands shook and her heart raced, and she wanted to throw up.

This felt like full-blown panic.

This was how she had felt when Jada kicked the table apart, drew his knife, and lunged for her. Like there was a clear, immediate threat in her face, right now. But there was nothing, nothing, nothing in her office....

The details of the office around her faded, and she caught glimpses of another scene.

Winter-bare trees, snow-covered ground, cold biting her lungs. The blow of a horse's gasp for breath. It had been running for too long.

Others shouting. *Ride faster!*

And: *If we try to go any faster, we'll kill Marcus!*

And a tree line, just below a ridge…

Warriors poured out of the tree line, a sickening number. Many were on horseback and hell-bent on pursuit.

A sharp burst of pain snapped her surroundings back into place again. Her elbow hurt, along with the back of her head. Sitting up, disoriented, it took her a moment to realize she had lost her balance and fallen.

She realized something else as well.

The goddess had never given her any visions based in the present. They had always been from possible outcomes in the future.

But not this time.

This time she had seen images of her people, and they were fighting to get home.

Chapter Ten

L EAPING TO HER feet, she raced out.

In the next room, Prem perched on the corner of her desk as she talked with a few of the older acolytes.

"Fetch my winter jacket, cloak, and gloves," she told them. "I need healers and Defenders to meet me down at the dock. Now." Then, as all three frozen women stared, she shouted at them, *"Run!"*

That galvanized them into action. Eyes wide, they scattered.

Lily raced down the halls and through courtyards. Urgency beat at her with frantic wings. It was quicker to cut through the temple, so she did. Voices rose behind her, calling out questions and exclamations.

"Your grace—what is it?"

"Is anything wrong?"

Then, from Margot down one hall: "Lily!"

She didn't stop for any of them. By the time she reached the wide stairs that led down to the great barred doors to the dock, she was flanked by three Defenders.

One of them, Justin, tried to give her his cloak, and she waved it away impatiently. The two others joined them as she plunged down the steps and ordered the doors be opened. Together they stared across the white expanse to the mainland.

"I don't think we can force the barges through that, your grace," one Defender told her.

She focused on Wulf's sentry on the mainland, but she couldn't communicate with them from that distance. The only way to get help to her people was by crossing the strait.

Go, Camael whispered.

She didn't pause to question it. There was no time to have a crisis of faith.

She ran.

"Your grace, wait—we haven't tested the ice yet!" Justin roared behind her. "Oh, flipping hells."

She ignored everything else—the biting wind, the cold that numbed her hands and face and sent stabs of pain shooting into her chest—and raced as fast as she could toward the shore. Wulf would help. She just had to get to him.

Once, her feet slipped out from underneath her and she would have fallen, but strong arms caught her. Giving her a wild-eyed look, Justin set her back on her feet again.

Glancing back at the abbey, she saw others following them. That was all she took the time to notice, for as soon as she regained her footing, she ran again.

Then, on the shore, she saw more soldiers gather. Some set out on the ice and raced toward her. One of them was Wulf.

He was among the fastest. His long legs tore over the distance, and his body in motion was a study in power and grace. She had never felt so glad to see anyone in her life.

As they neared, Justin drew his sword. Sparing him one exasperated glance, she snapped, "Hold, damn it!"

Trying to talk while running made her abused lungs protest. She sucked in a breath, and the dry, frigid air bit the back of her throat. As Wulf reached her, she bent over in a spasm of coughing.

He grasped her by the arms. "What's wrong?"

The only way she could speak was by telepathizing. *We need soldiers—horses—healers… We need to hurry!*

Whipping off his cloak, he wrapped her up, scooped her into his arms, and raced for shore.

"Gods damn it—your grace!" That was Justin who raced alongside them.

She was still coughing too hard to respond out loud, her throat raw while the muscles in her chest squeezed like a vise.

I'm all right, she told Justin. *He's helping. I don't want any of our people picking a fight with the Braugnes. Pass the word.*

Yes, your grace. Giving her an unhappy look, Justin started shouting at the other Defenders who drew near.

By the time Wulf climbed onto shore, she had caught her breath again, and he set her on her feet. Lionel appeared at his shoulder, along with Gordon and Jermaine. As she looked for Justin, she saw with gratitude that Estrella, the captain of her Defenders, had reached her side, and Margot too.

More Defenders were climbing to shore, along with priestesses carrying their healer packs. Even Prem joined them, clutching Lily's cloak and gloves, which she handed over wordlessly.

Wulf captured her attention. Looking up into his hard face, she saw the commander was present in full force.

"How many horses do we need?" he asked.

"I don't know."

He gave her a fierce frown. "Well, how many fighters and healers?"

"I don't know! How many is a lot?" Closing her eyes, she tried to bring back the image of the snowy countryside and the ridge behind the trees. "I know where we need to go. There's a ridge about five miles away, near a waterfall that's frozen right now."

Estrella said, "I'm familiar with that place."

Lily met Wulf's gaze. "We have a party with wounded who are trying to get to us. They're being pursued by many more troops than they had expected. I saw them pour out of the tree line. Our group is spent, and they aren't going to make it if we don't get there in time. I don't know how to gauge how many are after them, because I only got the images in flashes—but I'm going to guess over a hundred. Wulf, I want my people to come back home. Plan for much more."

He nodded and squeezed her arm then rapped out

orders, and soldiers leaped into action. A dozen cavalry, already mounted, danced on restless horses.

Wulf told Lily, "Every minute counts, you said. I'm going to send them ahead while the others muster. We just need to know where to go." Telepathically, he added, *Brace yourself. The advance scout will have a higher casualty rate.*

There would be time for grief later, when they knew how much this had cost them. Lily looked at Estrella. "Go with them."

"Yes, your grace!"

Estrella joined the party, and they plunged off.

After that, Lily figured the best thing she could do was get out of the way. She was a visionary, not a fighter. Within a remarkably short time, a much larger force comprised of Defenders, Braugne soldiers, and healers was assembled.

One short, intense argument punctuated the gathering when Wulf discovered Lily in the process of mounting a mare that one of the Defenders had brought to her. Eyes blazing, he snatched her horse's bridle.

"What do you think you're doing?" he snapped. "Stay here! You have no business putting yourself in danger."

Behind his preemptory attitude was a deep, genuine alarm. She didn't waste energy on getting angry. Instead, she asked, "Can you see the things that I can see?"

A single heartbeat passed, an intense throb of silence. Wulf's jaw clenched and his eyes blazed, and she could see just how badly he wanted to refute her. But she had him, and he knew it.

"Fine, you stay with me," he growled. "Right by me, do you hear? I want you close enough I can cut off anybody's head that tries to get to you."

Behind him, Lily saw Justin, Lionel, and Jermaine. Jermaine didn't appear to be surprised, but Lionel and Justin looked flabbergasted.

In a clear voice that carried to everyone nearby, she told Wulf, "Of course. You're the commander."

His dark gaze lit. He touched her knee. "You bet I am."

THEY RACED FOR the ridge and the frozen waterfall.

The advance party had met up with the fleeing wounded, and the group was in the process of being overrun when two hundred cavalry, comprised of both Defenders and Braugne, hammered down on the attackers.

For the first time in his life, Wulf led command from the sidelines. Not that there was much to do once the main body of troops arrived.

"They don't leave this battlefield," he said to Jermaine. "I don't want word of this getting back to Varian. We either capture them or we kill them."

"Understood, Commander."

Jermaine rode off to execute his orders, and in a complete reversal, what had begun as a rout quickly turned into a slaughter of the other side.

It was hard to stay on the sidelines. He couldn't deny it. But every time he felt the impulse to roar forward and engage with the enemy, he looked around for Lily. Her face was white and set while she watched the fray, her restless horse pacing back and forth.

And he couldn't do it. He couldn't leave her, not even when the most logical part of his brain insisted that she would be safe with a dozen fighters surrounding her. So he dealt with it. While the future might be a wide-open, unpainted canvas upon which they would make a multitude of other choices, for now the ones they'd made on that day were okay.

Even in the best scenario, the aftermath of battle was difficult. There were prisoners to control and question, the wounded and dying to tend, and, inevitably, they had casualties to identify.

Like their fighters, the abbey's healers worked side by side with the Braugne army doctors. Wulf knew they got lucky, and the casualty list was going to be as good as it got in times of war, but that didn't ease the stricken look on Lily's face as she dove into helping the healers.

Finally he couldn't stand it any longer. Pulling her away from the triage station, he said gently, "Go back now, love."

She gripped his shirt. "I can't just leave."

"Yes, you can. You can't be everything to everybody all the time, so don't even try, otherwise eventually it will kill you. Let everyone else do their jobs, and at least go back to one of the inns. I'm going to get a few questions answered, and then I'll meet you there."

She took a deep breath and let it out slowly. "All right. I'll see you back in town."

He kissed her lingeringly, right there, in front of his people and hers. Without looking, he heard everything around them grow quiet.

She sucked in a breath, but she didn't pull away. In fact, rather uncertainly, she kissed him back, and he counted that as a win too.

"Bold choice," she murmured against his lips. "Unexpected."

"Advance communiques are effective at disseminating new policy to a populace," he whispered, letting his fingertips linger on the soft curve of her cheek.

"Oh dear goddess, did you just say that to me?" Pulling back, she eyed him askance. "Was that remarkable sentence your way of flirting?"

He narrowed his eyes. "Of course not. The chocolate and the terrible orange food were my way of flirting. This was me making a public statement of intent. You'll know when I'm flirting again."

"Will I?" One corner of her lips tilted up. "What were you doing when you climbed my tower?"

He paused to consider. "Yes, that was flirting too."

"Re-eally. I thought that was you looking for an argument."

"It was an arguing kind of flirting," he told her. "Remember, I brought the orange food and the chocolate with me. And since you're going to bar your windows anyway, that was a singular event."

"I'm not going to bar my windows," Lily told him.

His voice hardened. "Unacceptable."

"Isssss it?" Her eyebrows rose slowly to her hairline. "Tough. That's my decision to make, because nobody in their right mind would make that climb, Wulf. Nobody except for you. And for your information, I was firm but very nice when I talked to Gennita this morning, and I offered her beautiful solutions to resolve our conflict. So you go ahead and do what you do, but you leave me to do what I do."

He had already recognized he wanted her, but that was the moment Wulf fell in love. Because he might take her, and she might give in to him, but he knew he would never succeed in conquering her.

Laying his hand against her cheek, he whispered softly, "Lily."

That was all, just *Lily*.

He knew his expression transmitted everything he was feeling, because he made no attempt to hide it. Her gaze softening, she put her hand over his.

When they finally drew apart, Margot swooped down on Lily like a bird of prey and bore her away, and *that* was a conversation Wulf was perfectly content to avoid. He plunged into work, and much later, he went to find her in town.

She hadn't been idle, he saw as he walked down the main street. The doors of several homes stood open, and from the glimpses of the interiors and the activity in the streets, the houses were being turned into temporary hospitals—an idea so superb and obvious he should have thought of it himself.

He found Lily in the Sea Lion, drinking wine and picking at a plate of food, with Defenders strategically placed throughout the taproom. Her tired face lit when she saw him.

Deliberately he walked over, bent, and kissed her on the lips. All movement and discussion in the room stopped, then slowly started up again.

"There," he said with satisfaction. "Now I've declared my intentions to your bodyguards and the townsfolk too."

There went those slender, expressive eyebrows again. They were excessively talented at telling him off, those eyebrows. No words were necessary, although that didn't stop her.

"You haven't declared anything to anyone, not least of all *to me*," she retorted. "All you've done is kiss me, and…" She held up both hands and laughed. "So what?"

"If I did not have a healthy self-esteem, I might take that the wrong way," he told her. He sat on the bench beside her, close enough their hips brushed, propped his elbow on the table and rested his head in his hand, and angled his body toward her.

When she laughed harder, he smiled. Then sobered. "Estrella has already given me her report. She said the weather mages were all dead, and that the attacking party was so large because they had been the focal point for the weather mages. The mages would split away from the main group to cast their spells and then meet up with them again afterward. That's what I know. What else do you have?"

"Your priestesses did well. After comparing accounts from several different prisoners with our own head count, I'm pretty certain we either captured or killed everyone in their group, which was what I was hoping for." After a brief pause, he added, "They're Guerlan, of course."

"Of course," she muttered. She shoved her plate of food over to him, and he ate hungrily. Shredding a heel of bread with restless fingers, she said, "Anything more?"

There was no way to make the next part easier. "From what we can gather, word was sent to Varian as soon as the first weather mages fell. He'll know soon enough that Calles was involved. They fought so hard to take your party before it got back to you because they didn't want Calles to know it was them."

"Everything he's done, he's tried to do in an underhanded way." Her mouth tightened.

"Yes," he said. "He's tried to take gold that wasn't his, and then he killed my brother in an attempt to cover it up. He's spread rumors about me and my troops, and killed people and set fire to their homesteads to create terror and resistance in every land we've passed through. He's poisoned my troops to slow us down and tried to assasinate me, and the weather mages were meant to either finish us off or drive us back to Braugne to wait out the winter."

Brushing aside the shredded crumbs of bread, she murmured, "He's working hard avoid meeting you on the battlefield."

"That's because he'll lose," he said flatly. There was not a shred of doubt in Wulf's soul about that. "Varian's living on borrowed time, and I think he knows it. Enough about him for now. I want to talk about you."

The wary look came back into her eyes. She said, "All riiiiiigght. What do you want to talk about?"

"Winter solstice is only a few days away now." Capturing one of her hands, he played with her fingers. "My men have marched across a continent. They've fought off magical attacks and poison, and they need a break, with something to look forward to. Does Calles celebrate the Masque?"

"We do," she told him, smiling. "In fact, there would already be decorations out in the streets except everyone evacuated to the abbey. Why, would you like to celebrate the Masque with us?"

Let Varian stew for a few days over the disappearance of his mages and troops. In the meantime, Wulf wanted to conduct another campaign that was of the utmost importance.

He returned her smile. "Yes, I would."

Chapter Eleven

I N MANY WAYS, it had been a grim day, but sparring with Wulf had made Lily feel a little bit better.

That evening, he escorted her back to the abbey despite her insistence that it was not necessary and that the half a dozen people who accompanied her were more than enough of an escort.

Halfway across the frozen strait, his gloved hand reached out and took hers. They walked the rest of the way hand in hand.

Once they arrived at the bottom of the stairs at the dock, he tugged her around to face him and kissed her. And kissed her.

And kissed her.

As he pulled her hood up around them, it gave them a sense of privacy that simply wasn't real, but she did appreciate the gesture.

His lips were so warm, and she knew them so well. She had kissed them in a thousand dreams.

As he drew back, she whispered, "If this is another advance communique to disseminate a new policy to a populace, I might smack you."

He gave her a shadowed grin. "No, love. This is me flirting again. Sleep well. I'll see you soon."

With reluctance obvious in his body language, he finally let her go and headed back across the strait. She watched his strong, solitary figure for a while, then peeked around the edge of her hood at the Defenders who guarded the open doors.

They stared straight ahead, expressions rigid. One particular Defender's eyes bulged slightly, clearly from some kind of internalized pressure, while his psyche rolled around and laughed.

Facing Margot had been difficult enough. Deciding she didn't have to emerge from the depths of her hood if she didn't want to, Lily hid from curious gazes as she hurried up to her tower where she slept like the dead the entire night.

The next morning, before Lily'd had a chance to drink her first cup of tea, Gennita found her and said she and her husband had decided to stay. While the older woman was awkward, Lily could see that Gennita's psyche had softened significantly, so she accepted the news gladly.

A few hours later, after interviewing Dulcinda and Evie, she appointed Dulcinda as her second secretary, dumped the budget into her hands, and said, "Please come back to me with this pared down to the bare essentials. We're going to hold on to as much coin as we can in case we need to buy more food before the next harvest."

"I'd be delighted to, your grace."

After delegating the budget to someone else, Lily felt like such a renegade she scooped up the rest of the requests for priestesses and put those on Prem's desk.

"I want your best recommendations for these," she told Prem.

"Yes, your grace!" Beaming at her, Prem got to work.

Your grace. It made her feel so old. Just as she turned away, Estrella strode into the outer office. While the captain of the Defenders wore an entirely appropriate expression, her psyche was tinged red with anger as it glared at Lily.

"Good morning, your grace," Estrella said. "Your invader is here."

"My… invader." With an effort, Lily forced herself to stop staring at the area over Estrella's head.

"Yes, your grace. You know, the one who killed his brother and burned farms and murdered families, then marched his army unasked onto our land and started kissing you. That one."

Breathing deeply, Lily rubbed her face. Calm, be calm.

She told Estrella, "He didn't kill his brother. The king of Guerlan did. He didn't do any of the other things either. Well, he did march his army unasked onto our land, and… he did start kissing me. But the rest of it isn't true."

Some of the anger in Estrella's psyche faded. Frowning, she asked, "Are you sure?"

"You know how good my truthsense is. Yes, I am."
She looked over her fingers at the captain. "What does
he want?"

"He has requested an audience with you. After
yesterday, none of the Defenders are entirely sure how
we're supposed to respond to his presence. He walked
across from the mainland by himself, so he doesn't pose
an immediate threat—"

"Captain, he's not a threat to us, not unless we do
something stupid like endanger him or any of his men,
and we're not going to do that." She drummed her
fingers. "I have invited him to stay through winter
solstice. The Braugnes are to be treated with courtesy
and welcomed to our Masque. Please tell the townsfolk
they are still welcome to stay at the abbey, but those who
wish to return home may do so with my blessing."

The tension in Estrella's shoulders eased. "Yes, your
grace. I'll see that word gets out to the evacuees. About
the invad—about the Protector of Braugne. Shall I turn
him away?"

"No, please show him to my office." As Estrella left,
Lily looked at Prem and said, "He promised me flirting.
This should be good."

Glee danced in Prem's eyes. "Oh, your grace, that's
amazing. Do... do we welcome it?"

"That depends entirely on what he does." Shrugging,
Lily walked back into her office and waited.

She looked out the window until, behind her, Estrella
said, "The Protector of Braugne, your grace."

Lily turned, but the words she had prepared in greeting died unspoken as Wulf strode across the room to her. He looked the same, a powerfully built, hardened man wearing armor, cloak, and sword, but in one hand he held a large bouquet of vivid red roses.

For a moment the illusion held perfectly. She even caught a whiff of scent that smelled like roses. Then, as he drew closer and she stared, she realized the bouquet he held was made of the velvet roses from the shop he had broken into.

Smiling, she held out her hands for them. "They're beautiful—thank you. I swear I even smell roses."

"I sprinkled perfume on the blooms." As he gave them to her, he bent in to steal a swift kiss. Warming with pleasure, she kissed him back.

"I take it you added more money to the jar behind the counter."

Smiling faintly, he said, "Did you doubt me?"

"Not at all." She buried her face in the soft velvet blooms, inhaled with pleasure, then set them aside. "I also checked the shop yesterday afternoon when I returned to town. It was exactly as you had said. The coin has remained undisturbed. In fact, I think there was even more than what you originally put there."

"Of course."

Leaning back against her desk, she asked, "What can I do for you, Wulf?"

"If you can spare an hour, I would like for you to give me a tour of the abbey. From all accounts I've read, it's a beautiful place. I'd like to hear the things you love about it."

She lit up even further. "Let me get my cloak."

They walked through the grounds and the temple while they talked. He tucked her hand into the crook of his arm, and she allowed it.

Not everyone welcomed the sight of them together. While they were greeted with infallible politeness, the psyches of some glared at them with fear and hatred because people were people, and even though Wulfgar was not responsible for the violence that had come to Calles, it had still come because of his presence. And change was hard.

At the end of the hour, they paused at the top of the steps that led to the dock. Looking down at her, his expression serious, he said, "It's as beautiful as everyone said."

"I think so." She frowned as she tried to gain clues about his change in mood. The wolf in his psyche had turned away from her, head down.

Kissing her mouth and then her cheek, he told her, "I'll see you soon."

When he left, he took the brightness out of the wintery day and what warmth there was with him. She watched him walk back to the mainland where a cadre of his soldiers stood vigil. Once he joined them, they moved away, back to the army camp.

That set the pattern for the next few days. The next day whenWulf returned, he brought ancient manuscripts.

"Ooooh, the ancient manuscripts," Lily said while she rubbed her hands together in delight. "Wait, those were supposed to be a bribe."

"They were not a bribe! They were a gift. You were just too afraid of me to accept them."

"I wasn't afraid of you! I went into your army camp all by myself, didn't I? It was the politics, the appearance of supporting one side over another."

He laughed. "Well, that ship has sailed, hasn't it? Take them, love, and enjoy them with my welcome."

That ship had, indeed, sailed.

"Thank you." Smiling, she accepted the gift. "I will."

He always kissed her in greeting, and he never failed to kiss her when he left. It made her happy, but restless too. A hunger for him developed. It scratched at her underneath her skin and made her toss and turn at night.

Once, she opened up the window with the broken latch just to glare down at the pitons that ran down the side of the tower and were clearly not used enough.

Meanwhile, many of the townsfolk migrated back into town, and decorations began to appear. Calles was beautiful in midwinter, with the lights glowing in the houses and shops and brightly colored banners and ribbons festooning the doors and windows of every building.

The abbey decorated for the holiday too. It was always such a deep pleasure to pull out with reverence the ornaments and decorations that were generations old. The Masque was a celebration of all the gods—those

that were called the gods of the Elder Races on Earth—
and not just Camael, so they set up representations for
all seven.

As god of the Dance, Taliesin always came first. Half
male and half female, Taliesin was first among the Primal
Powers because everything dances, the planets and all the
stars, the other gods, the Elder Races, and humans.
Dance is change, and the universe is constantly in
motion.

There was also Azrael, the god of Death; Inanna, the
goddess of Love; Nadir, the goddess of the depths or the
Oracle; Will, the god of the Gift; Hyperion, the god of
Law, and, of course, Camael, goddess of the Hearth.

As she helped set out the decorations, Lily fussed
extra long over Camael's arrangement in the temple,
whispering to the goddess, "Because I'm partial."

As a gentle waft of air passed through the temple,
she thought she caught a hint of the goddess's smile.

In Calles, the Masque was held in town. The
procession of the gods passed down the main street, and
then those who wanted to participate opened their doors
for the evening.

Music played on street corners, everyone danced,
several people drank too much, and sometimes a couple
of fights broke out because of it, but overall, the Masque
was always tremendous fun.

The day before, Jermaine and Lionel came to meet
with Estrella and Margot about how best to provide
security. As much as people had relaxed to enjoy the

moment, nobody had forgotten that a war had just begun.

Afterward, Margot brought the plan to Lily to approve. "Since the Braugnes will be pulling out of Calles the day after the Masque, Jermaine said the commander wants to leave an armed presence in the town—he said it's for our protection." Margot searched her gaze. "Have you already talked this over with Wulfgar?"

For a moment, Lily lost her breath. Then, very carefully, she straightened a few papers on her desk while a fine tremor ran through her fingers.

"No," she replied. "We haven't discussed any of that."

Margot covered her hand. "What's going on?"

I have no idea, she wanted to say. He touches my face and... and when he kisses me, his mouth feels desperate. But his wolf has turned away from me. He has changed his mind, and I don't know why.

Clearing her throat, she said, "I think accepting an armed presence is a good idea. If Varian decides to retaliate for our stopping his weather mages, our force is too small to defend the town on our own."

"I agree." Margot shook her head. "And if you had asked me that two weeks ago, I would have said *oh hell no.*"

Lily gave her a twisted smile. "I used to think the goddess wanted me to make some kind of grand, big choice that would take us down either one path or another. Now I think we all face a series of choices every day—explore this, don't do that. Choose to do the right thing or the wrong one. Agree to work together. Break the law. And our lives become the sum of each chosen moment. You know, I almost decided to go to Guerlan for the Masque, but when I read Varian's invitation, I knew we were going to be facing a hard winter, and I didn't want to spend the money."

Margot shuddered. "I'm so glad you didn't go."

"Me too." Looking down at her desk, Lily said, "The plans are sound, both for security for the Masque tomorrow night and for what happens when the army leaves. I approve."

After Margot left, Lily gave up trying to work and ascended her tower to sit and watch the flames in the hearth. Her thoughts formed, spun, and reformed, and like a kaleidoscope, the landscape changed, depending on how she looked at it.

The future was always full of an almost infinite number of potential paths. Just because she had dreamed of a life with Wulf, that didn't ensure it would happen. She, of all people, should have remembered that.

For the first time she realized she hadn't seen any visions for the past several days.

Maybe that was because, for the goddess, the critical choice had already been made. Maybe it had never been about picking either of the two men who even now were at war with each other.

Maybe the critical decision had always been about

the fight to save innocent lives, choosing to take action to stop the weather mages and accepting whatever consequences that came because of it.

If that were so, it might be enough to satisfy Camael, but it wasn't enough for Lily.

Wulf didn't come to visit that day.

Chapter Twelve

THE MASQUE IN Calles the next evening was delightful in every sense of the word.

Bonfires, placed at strategic places, provided golden light and heat for anyone who needed to warm up in the middle of festivities. The foundling children from the abbey played with the townsfolk children on the ice while smiling guardians watched over them.

Musicians played on almost every street corner, and the food—dear gods, the food. The abbey hauled cartfuls of both sweet and savory pastries across the strait along with roasted turkeys and hams and baskets full of fresh apples. The shops remained open, and the food merchants sold their wares, but the largesse from the abbey was free to all. Everyone assured Wulf that they had cut back on extravagances that year. The inhabitants of Calles knew very well that they were still facing a difficult winter.

But to the men who had been eating camp rations for weeks, it was a veritable feast, and there was plenty of ale for purchase at both inns. Still, eight thousand troops was a lot for a relatively small town to absorb, so the

Braugne soldiers passed through in rotation, giving everyone a chance to dance, eat, and drink a little before the night was through.

Not everyone wore masks. Jermaine had forbidden any of the troops to disguise their faces. The security risk was too elevated. But many of the townsfolk, and those from the abbey, wore costumes and masks.

After all, there was a touch of romance to be had in dancing with the butcher's wife, who pretended to hide her identity behind a pretty mask of peacock feathers. Or the Sea Lion's innkeeper who wore a horned stag's head but who still gave himself away with his booming laugh.

The whole event, set against the backdrop of snow, was so damn charming and picturesque Wulf was wild to get out of there.

He was ready to go. His possessions were packed. Both Karre and Mignez had sent the troops they had promised in their treaties, and six thousand men waited for him at the juncture where Calles's border met Guerlan's. His own army would march in the morning, but Wulf planned on going on ahead with a smaller party that night.

There was just one thing that kept him from leaving.

Lily hadn't made her appearance yet.

He stood at the mouth of the alley by the Sea Lion, leaning against the corner of the building, arms crossed, as his restless gaze roamed over the crowd.

Then children ran down the streets, shrieking, "It's time! It's time!"

People hurried to move back from the center of the street, making way for the procession of the gods. The person who played the part of Taliesin came first, leaping and twirling as they made their way down the street, dressed in a costume that made them appear to be half man, half woman.

Then the other gods walked past, each in costumes that portrayed their roles—Death, Love, the Oracle, the god of the Gift, and Law.

And last came the goddess of the Hearth, and of course it was Lily. Dressed in a golden gown that simulated flames, her dark hair pinned up behind the mask of a beautiful, smiling woman, she looked otherworldly and magnificent, and the entire crowd—the Braugnes, the townsfolk, and the abbey alike—roared in joy.

Wulf didn't raise his voice with the others. When he saw her, his chest constricted, and a pain swept over him that was so fierce it almost drove him to his knees.

When Lily walked past, she looked at him, and the gold of her costume caught in her eyes.

He had thought to say goodbye to her at the Masque. He hadn't taken into account how everyone would swarm her when the procession of the gods had ended. With a slight, bitter smile, he watched the large knot of laughing people. She was lost in the middle of it, too petite for him to see.

Very well, he would write her a farewell letter instead. Perhaps it was better that way.

He said to Gordon, who hovered nearby, "I'm headed back to camp. Tell the rest of our party we'll leave in an hour."

Gordon nodded. "Yes, sir."

After Wulf walked back, he lit a lamp, dug out the chest that contained his writing materials, and sat at the table. For a long while, he stared at an empty page, pen at the ready, but what could he say?

I wanted you more than anything, and then I loved you.

And then I saw how much you love your beautiful home, and I loved you too much to take you away from it.

Closing his eyes, he put his head in his hands.

From the direction of the tent flap, Lily said, "All ready to leave, I see."

He had heard nothing, not even the sound of the tent flap being disturbed. Her cloaking spell was that good.

Astonishment roared. He surged to his feet. "Seven hells!"

She walked in, her expression set. Her hair was still pinned high, but she had shed the golden costume. Like him, she wore black—black riding boots, trousers, quilted vest. Even her gloves and cloak were black.

She tore off her gloves and slapped them on the table. "You were going to leave, just like that—with no goodbye?" Her gaze fell on his pen and paper, and her mouth took on a bitter twist. "Well, maybe a note. Wulf, it's going to be a long time before I forgive you for that."

Gods, he needed to kiss her, and kiss her. To tear off her clothes and make love to her with all the anguished hunger in his heart until it wrecked them both.

Spinning away, he ran his hands through his hair. "I was going to talk to you tonight."

"At the Masque."

"Yes, but I should have realized how inundated you would be by everyone. So yes, I was going to write you a letter."

"Asshole," she whispered unsteadily.

When he looked over his shoulder, she had tears in her eyes and she looked so betrayed it felt like he took a knife to the chest.

Good. Let her feel betrayed. That might put a quicker end to this torture.

"I love you," he said.

"I know you do!" she snapped. "So what? I love you too, and I would never leave you like this!"

The distance between them grew intolerable. Striding over to her, he gripped her arms and said fiercely into her face, "I love you, and I'm in a war that has only just begun, and this camp? Lily, this camp is the best you will ever see it. It smells clean, doesn't it? It smells fresh, because everything is frozen. Over the next few years, there's going to be more mud and blood, and danger and stink, than you can possibly imagine, and the battles are going to be brutal and gut-wrenching. Meanwhile, you have an amazing home filled with a richness of history that you love passionately, and a people who adore you. You have a place, and a function, and your *hearth* is here."

As he spoke, the tears in her eyes spilled over and slipped down her face. "Yes, I do," she said. "I love this place passionately. That's why I've been grooming Margot as prime minister for the past six months— because I wanted to leave the abbey and Calles in the best, most capable hands when I left."

Stricken, he whispered, "Lily, what are you saying?"

She slapped his chest and cried, "I'm saying you don't get to take my choices away from me, and I choose you, Wulf! I choose you, and not over Guerlan. Over my home."

The enormity of that silenced him.

Then he said simply, "You can walk away from the abbey, just like that?"

"Not quite just like that." The light threw deep shadows under her eyes. "I was up all night, but… yes."

"My gods, love, that's so much for you to sacrifice." Her shining hair was beginning to slip out of the pins. He brushed the fine strands back from her face. "When I began that letter, I was going to ask you to wait for me. If you couldn't, then I would have to accept it, because this is going to take so gods damned long—"

Nodding, she swiped at her nose. "So I should take my bags and tent, my twenty-five healer priestesses, two assistants, and my two hundred and fifty Defenders, and I should go back home, get over you, and fall in love with another man. Sure, Wulf. Okay."

Wait, what?

What other man?!

"What are you saying now?" he roared. For the first time, he took in the implications of her outfit. She walked everywhere around the abbey and town, but she was dressed in riding boots. Realization struck. "You packed. You prepared for this. You're ready to go."

She met his gaze, her mouth set. "That's right, Wulf. I'm ready to go. And I'm not going to wait for you. Either I come with you now, or I walk away. I'm not going to sit at home and worry and pine over you for years. You're a stupid man, so I hate to say this, but it's your decision."

"Lily," he breathed.

Forget about the miracles that danced like fireflies around her. She was a miracle so enormous he clenched her against his chest for fear she might disappear on him again. Her arms wound around his waist, and she clenched him tightly too.

Burying his face in her hair, he said, "You make me want to be better than I am. So I was trying to be a better man."

"I didn't fall in love with a better man," she whispered. "I fell in love with you."

Faced with the enormity of her choice and the depth of her feelings, there was only one thing he could say. Only one thing he had ever wanted to say.

"Stay. It's going to be hard, but stay the course, you

beautiful, brave woman. Stay with me." He tilted up her face and kissed her. "You're so much more than I deserve."

She slipped a hand to the back of his neck. "That goes without saying."

He kissed her again, and again. The soft, rich curves of her mouth captivated him. "Are you going to be scolding me for a while?"

She met him kiss for kiss. "That too goes without saying. It might take me a month or two."

"Whatever you need to do, my love." Unbuttoning her jacket, he cupped her soft breast and gritted his teeth. "Gods, I want you."

"I want you t—" she began, but just then the tent flap lifted.

"Sir, we're ready to go," Gordon said as he stepped in. "Did you know we also have quite a few priestesses and Defenders waiting at the edge of… camp…?"

Wulf froze, then withdrew his hand slowly from her breast. Looking deeply into his eyes, Lily smiled. She said telepathically, *This is only the first of many, many interruptions I foresee in our future.*

Thank the goddess I'm in love with a woman who knows how to protect her boundaries. As her smile widened, he turned to Gordon and said aloud, "Change of plans. We will head out in the morning with the rest of the troops. Please see that the priestesses and Defenders are given a suitable area to camp for the night. Her grace will need some of her people nearby, but we'll figure out where everybody belongs in formation tomorrow. That will be all for tonight, Gordon."

Ducking his head, Gordon said to the ground, "Good night, sir, your grace."

Wulf looked at Lily. "I just disposed of you again."

"Clearly you're going to need some training…" She gasped as he hauled her against him and drove his mouth down over hers. He delved deeply, spearing her with his tongue, while urgency beat in the drumming of his blood.

Her tongue dueled with his as her fingers flew over him, first unbuttoning his coat, then his shirt. Pulling away, he yanked them off. The tent was cold, the braziers unlit. His bed had been stripped, the blankets and furs rolled. Everything about this was raw and inelegant, and none of it mattered.

While he grabbed a rolled-up blanket and shook it out, she tore out of her clothes. She turned to him, completely nude, and the sight of her gorgeous body made the flames of his hunger leap hotter, higher.

Wrapping her up in the blanket, he grabbed both their cloaks and steered her backward to the bed pallet while her hands roamed greedily over the bare expanse of his chest.

He was so hard and aching and hot for her. He said between his teeth, "Tell me now, love—how careful should I be?"

For a moment her face went blank, but then she grasped his meaning. "I'm no virgin, Wulf. You don't need to coax me along."

That's what he needed to know. Thrusting her backward onto the pallet, he fell on top of her. Good gods, how had she not been snapped up by someone else? He was going to find every single one of her ex-lovers and grind their faces into dust—no, wait, that was probably unbalanced...

He had to touch her everywhere, taste every curve and hollow, and while he feasted all over her body, she undulated underneath his hands, grasping and stroking and licking him until the fire burned so hot he could only quench it by penetrating deep within her.

They discovered their own rhythm together, and it was the best of all dances, and the give and the take, the gasp of breath, the exquisite peak of pleasure and sigh of release, all of it played the beat to which they danced.

He was shaking when he finished. She had gone before him, and so she held him with her whole body, her arms and legs wrapped tightly around him. As he looked down into her eyes, he stroked the damp hair off her face.

Heart still pounding, still inside her, he whispered, "I'll hurt you again, but I will always be sorry when I do it. I'll try not to, but that's not how life works."

"No, it isn't," she whispered back.

"I will swear to you this—I'll always be true to you." He stared down at her fiercely. "Always."

As she stared at him, he had just enough time to wonder what she saw. When a smile brightened her face, it was like watching the sun rise in the morning.

"Yes," she said. "I can see that you will."

He could do no less. She was his miracle, and the gods only knew, not very many people got the chance to have one.

Using both cloaks, they settled together as tightly as they could. Tomorrow there would be challenges. A war to fight, an empire to build.

But there were always challenges.

There would also be the chance to dance with her again.

And before he fell asleep, Wulf wondered if maybe there wasn't an end to any story.

Maybe there is only, ever, just the beginning.

Thank you!

Dear Readers,

Thank you for reading *The Chosen*! I hope you enjoyed Wulf's and Lily's story as much as I enjoyed writing it.

Would you like to stay in touch and hear about new releases? You can:

- Sign up for my monthly email at: www.theaharrison.com
- Follow me on Twitter at @TheaHarrison
- Like my Facebook page at facebook.com/TheaHarrison

Reviews help other readers find the books they like to read. I appreciate each and every review, whether positive or negative.

Happy reading!
~Thea

Look for these titles from Thea Harrison

Pia Does Hollywood
Liam Takes Manhattan
Planet Dragos
The Chosen

GAME OF SHADOWS SERIES
Published by Berkley

Rising Darkness
Falling Light

ROMANCES UNDER THE NAME AMANDA CARPENTER

E-published by Samhain Publishing
(original publication by Harlequin Mills & Boon)
*These stories are currently out of print

A Deeper Dimension
The Wall
A Damaged Trust
The Great Escape
Flashback
Rage
Waking Up
Rose-Coloured Love
Reckless
The Gift of Happiness
Caprice
Passage of the Night
Cry Wolf
A Solitary Heart
The Winter King

Lightning Source UK Ltd.
Milton Keynes UK
UKHW020716220519
343123UK00007B/131/P

9 781947 046924